He took her by surprise when he reached out and tucked a finger under her chin, looked at her steady in the eyes.

Her breath caught and she couldn't move.

"I came all the way from the big city and have to tell you to relax, Willa?" he said quietly.

She didn't know what to say. Obviously he could tell she was tense and nervous and on edge. Admitting *he* was what was making her so tense and nervous and on edge wouldn't help matters, either.

"You're about to get offended now, aren't you?" he said. He let his hand drop.

He wasn't touching her anymore, and damn, she'd liked it. Just that teeny, tender touch. She'd *liked* it.

She swallowed hard. "No."

"All right," he said, his voice still soft. "Then I'm making progress, aren't I?"

"Progress to what?" she blurted out. Not a question she should really be asking, but there it was. She wanted to know the answer.

Dear Reader,

Something supernatural this way comes…. Anything can happen in one tiny West Virginia mountain town where an earthquake triggered positive ions and a wave of paranormal activity. In *High-Stakes Homecoming*, Penn Ramsey comes home to Haven to claim the old family farm…only someone else has already claimed it—and she's one tough competitor in this battle of opposing wills. Willa North is also the love that broke his heart, and soon they're mysteriously trapped in the old farmhouse together. Is the house enchanted, or is someone with a secret agenda terrorizing them both? Only by discovering the truth can they hope to survive….and claim the happiness together that is their true inheritance.

This book, in part, as are all the HAVEN books, is based on my own farm in the hills of West Virginia—though I hope nothing this scary ever happens here! It's far, far more fun to simply imagine, and I hope you'll come with me as you open the pages of this book.

Romantic, chilling and otherworldly…welcome back to Haven, WV!

Love,

Suzanne McMinn

SUZANNE McMINN

High-Stakes Homecoming

Silhouette®
Romantic
SUSPENSE

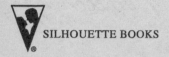

SILHOUETTE BOOKS

Recycling programs
for this product may
not exist in your area.

ISBN-13: 978-0-373-27632-5
ISBN-10:   0-373-27632-X

HIGH-STAKES HOMECOMING

Visit Silhouette Books at www.eHarlequin.com

Printed in U.S.A.

SUZANNE McMINN

lives by a lake in North Carolina with her husband and three kids, plus a bunch of dogs, cats and ducks. Visit her Web site at www.SuzanneMcMinn.com to learn more about her books, newsletter and contests. Check out www.paxleague.com for news, info and fun bonus features connected to her PAX League series about paranormal super agents!

Chapter 1

Coming back to West Virginia would be a big mistake.

The anonymous text message he'd received on his cell phone just that morning came back into Penn Ramsey's mind at the exact moment he slammed on his brakes, barely avoiding a six-point buck leaping across the rough, rock-based road, and just as barely avoiding a skid off a sheer, thirty-foot drop in the process. The haunting backcountry, with its thick, wild woods and narrow, twisting byways, was as unforgiving as it was forbidding. Rookie mistake, swerving to spare a deer's life, when the maneuver could cost your own.

Yeah, coming home was a mistake. He couldn't argue with that one.

He stared at the buck, where it had stopped frozen in his high beams. A tight beat passed, and then the animal turned, bounded madly up the opposite bank, and disappeared. Penn wondered again who would have sent him that cryptic message, a message that was either a mysterious note of concern or a sinister and veiled threat. He couldn't come up with an answer now, any more than he could while he'd been sitting on the plane.

Penn waited an impatient beat to make sure Bambi didn't have company. Despite his mistake, he had grown up in the country, and where there was one deer, there was often another. When none appeared, he pressed the gas. The rented Land Rover bounced on the rugged road. It was just starting to rain, and fog slid phantom fingers across the narrow lane as he came around the next bend.

New York City's blinking neon, blaring horns, and skyscraping buildings seemed a planet away. The countryside outside Haven, West Virginia, was as he remembered from his childhood, some kind of lushly-forested alternate universe, filled with memories and ghosts, overgrown hills and meadows—and quiet. Way too much quiet.

Quiet in which to remember, reflect; to once again experience guilt.

The fog cleared and he spied a porch light down below the road, saw the mailbox with its cheap, stick-on gold numbers and letters flash in his headlights. The box leaned over as if it had been run into one too many times, but the address remained— 2489 Laurel Run Road.

He was four miles from Limberlost Farm, he knew that now. He knew that because he knew exactly how far it was from the old family place to 2489 Laurel Run.

A big, old black walnut tree stood in a curve two miles up, halfway between Limberlost and that house on Laurel Run. The sweet spot. He and pretty Willa used to meet there when he was young and dumb and full of…

He slowed the Land Rover as fog rolled over the road again, windshield wipers slapping at the persistent drizzle outside the vehicle. He passed the black walnut tree as the fog swept in and out, playing chicken with the road. Willa'd gotten married and moved to town, last he heard. Granddad was dead. He'd kept in touch with a couple of his old football buddies for a while, but he'd lost track of them a long time ago.

He'd bet he didn't know a soul on Laurel Run these days. Not that many souls remained, from what he knew. He hadn't seen a porch light since he'd passed Willa's old place, and it was at least four miles since he'd left town after stopping for gas, and had turned down this godforsaken, unpaved road to nowhere.

You can't go home again. But here he was.

Turning around sounded real good.

The mist cleared away again, long enough for him to see in his beams that, yeah, the bank still fell off sharply to his left and the hill rose just as steeply to his right. No escape. He had a purpose here, and he couldn't leave till it was done.

Limberlost Farm, its four hundred acres, orchards, fields, ponds and river frontage, was worth something; maybe not a whole lot in a backwater town like Haven, but something. And all he had to do was live in the ramshackle of a farmhouse—that was likely halfway falling off the hill by now—for thirty days before he could sell it. Seed money, that's what he needed. Limberlost was his seed money.

Damn his cousin, Jess, for getting the money up front in the will. Penn got stuck with the property and its encumbering requirement of a month's residency to claim his inheritance. He would have fought the ridiculous requirement, but the executor of the estate had warned him that would only complicate the probate process. Penn could complete the month's requirement before the will even reached the probate judge. Bottom line, he wanted the money. Whatever would get him there quickest.

He'd been the top-producing marketing director at Brown and Sons Ltd. when he handed in his resignation, but he wasn't a Brown or a Son. Launching his own firm wasn't just a dream anymore. One month of hell. It was worth it. Then he'd put the place up for sale and take whatever he was offered. *Good riddance.*

He fought a burst of guilt. He had a right to live

his life the way he saw fit. He might have been born here, but he'd gotten out as soon as he could.

The farm shouldn't be much farther. At least, if he remembered correctly. The wildly wooded bank to his left leveled out as he came down the last rolling hill, where the road would reach the bottom land and open pasture. He saw teetering fence posts, slumping wire. The dark, the gloam, the decaying rural scenery—it was right out of a horror movie.

He saw a flash of light in the mist. An animal sprang onto the road ahead. A calf, this time.

Fog curled in sharp again, blinding him.

He hit the brakes, but the car only picked up speed as it ran down the slope. He slammed harder on the brakes, uselessly—adrenaline shot through his veins. He couldn't see, couldn't stop—

No brakes.

The fog cleared. The calf stood straight ahead, staring into his headlights, frozen. Penn swung the wheel to the right. The calf bolted, in the same direction. Penn veered to the other side and—

All he knew was, that wasn't a calf he struck.

It was a woman.

Willa hit hard, flat on her back. Sprinkles dotted her face. Rain. She lay there for a timeless stretch, aware of only the ominous sound of the growing storm around her. Wind. Cold.

Hands grabbed her shoulders, strong, urgent.

"Are you all right?"

She blinked, desperately working to clear her vision, pushing back tears that sprang out of nowhere. Reaction setting in, almost impossible to believe. Hit. She'd been hit. By a car.

His car. This stranger. She could see nothing of his face, just the gleam of his eyes. Her pulse thumped, kicking into gear out of shock. His voice sounded distantly familiar. Confusion left her blank, even as something deep inside clanged a warning she couldn't quite grasp.

Beneath her, she felt the rough rubble of the road. She struggled to make sense of her surroundings, remember where she was. *The broken fence. The calf. Then—*

That car, out of nowhere. Oh, God.

Sick horror gripped her. She pushed up with her hands, fighting past the arms that tried to hold her down. She had to see if she was okay, she had to see if anything was broken. She didn't have time to not be okay. She had the farm, Birdie, everything—too much. And it was all on her, by herself.

Relief nearly collapsed her backward when she realized her arms and legs were all right.

"I'm okay," she cried, pushing at the stranger holding her again. "Let go of me! I have to get my calf!"

"Forget your damn calf!" he grated back angrily. "You were just hit by a car! We need to get you to a hospital to be checked out!"

Where was her flashlight? Headlights framed the stranger bending over, leaving his face in darkness. Headlights from some sort of sport utility vehicle that was even now rammed into the stone pillar at the side of her gate. Fabulous. He'd nearly hit her calf, hit her, then hit her gatepost. She was lucky he hadn't plowed through the fence she'd just finished fixing, or plowed into her while she'd still been fixing it.

Her truck, her beat-up old Ford pickup truck, was still parked in the drive, undamaged. *Thank God.* She needed her truck.

Rain splashed down on them, harder now. She had to get her calf in. She had to get back up the hill to the house. Her four-year-old daughter was there, alone, waiting for her.

"Get off me!" she yelled, pushing against him with more strength now, even as his firm hands moved up and down her arms, down her body, as if checking her over. She didn't need checking over. Not by a hospital, and certainly not by him. "I'm fine."

She scrambled to her feet, managing to slip out from under him with a sudden move. She *was* fine. She was standing. Dazed, aware of an aching throb through her body, and fearsome rumblings of thunder from the dark sky above. It would be pouring soon.

He came after her, seeming taller and bigger with every step. She almost choked because she'd forgotten to swallow. It wasn't just his voice. His shape and form were frighteningly familiar. She felt a wave of dizzy fear that made no sense. She couldn't know him. She hadn't been expecting anyone.

"I still say you should be checked out at a hospital," the man said again. "You could have a concussion." He raised his voice over the buffeting wind.

She struggled to keep her feet, even as her knees wobbled. "I'm fine," she repeated. "And I don't really care what you say. I stood up too fast, that's all." She didn't want to admit that maybe she was just a little scared of him, or that her dizzy, sick sensation meant anything at all. She turned slowly, looking for her flashlight. She spotted it at the edge of his beams and went for it.

It was dead, totally dead. She'd dropped it when he hit her, along with the pliers, hammer and staples she'd been using to fix the fence. She reached down and grabbed the rope halter she'd brought to get the calf in.

Swinging around, she looked into the fog swirling past the road, swathing the bank. Her pulse thumped painfully. *Dammit, dammit, dammit.* She couldn't afford to lose anything, including that calf. Limberlost Farm was on a perpetual brink of disaster.

"Calf's gone. You'll find it tomorrow."

She swung back at him, irritated mostly because he was right. And arrogant about it.

"Would you leave me alone? Get in your car! Go away! Or get me your insurance information." How disoriented was she? She'd almost forgotten that vital point. "You hit my gatepost."

Not that it was some fabulous gatepost. It was old and crumbly. Whatever. He'd run into it.

"I hit *you,* too."

"I know that! I'm not going to the hospital. I don't need to. Nothing's broken. Just tell me who your insurance people are and your name and back your car on out of here."

"I'm not going anywhere," he said.

Her pulse thumped again. She stepped toward him. He stood just at the edge of the beams. God, he sounded familiar. And *looked* familiar in that edge of light…. Sheer instinct made her want to shrink back, but she didn't shrink from anyone, not anymore.

Dangerous, that's how he looked. Tall, powerfully built, dressed in jeans and a dark T-shirt under a leather jacket. Athletic shoes, not boots. He didn't look like he was from around here, or sound like it either, and yet his voice rang a bell. His face was all sharp planes and angles cut in shadows. She couldn't make out the details of his face, but she was almost positive he was good-looking. He was arrogant, wasn't he?

He definitely looked big and bad, which made her attempt to play at big and bad herself rather emptily.

"What do you mean?"

"My brakes. They're dead. That's why I couldn't stop the car. I tried not to hit the calf and…"

He'd hit her when she'd run into the road after it. Stupid move on her part. She was lucky to be alive, lucky he hadn't more than struck her with the corner of his bumper, which was just enough to knock her down. He'd swerved into her gatepost to keep from hitting her dead-on. Or she might be…dead.

Then her brain kicked in and she realized what he'd just said. His brakes had failed. He couldn't get out of here in his car. It was dark and rainy and late.

And stranded. Just what she needed to top off her evening. A stranded stranger.

"Where were you going?" As if she felt like ferrying him anywhere. But she couldn't leave him here at the side of the road under these conditions. Even if he had just hit her and damaged her property and seriously annoyed the hell out of her.

He jerked his head at the drive. "Here."

"Uh, what?"

"Limberlost Farm."

"Why?"

"Because it's mine."

Double blink. Had her hearing been affected?

"You're mistaken."

"I don't think so."

Now she forgot to breathe for a full beat. What was going on here?

"This is *my* farm," she said. Rain, soaking her now. She didn't care. Who was he? She was just about to ask that question but he beat her to it.

"Who are *you?*" he asked, and stepped toward her into the light from his beams.

Fully into the light.

Before she could open her mouth, he answered for her, his voice oh-so-familiar, and she knew exactly why. Oh yeah, she knew why he was so familiar and why she was so scared. Her head reeled.

"Willa?"

Chapter 2

Total panic, that's what Penn read in Willa's eyes. Willa...North these days. She'd married Jared North. Five weeks and three days after Penn had left Haven, not that he'd counted or cared or paid much attention at the time. *Liar.*

But he'd certainly made a heroic effort to forget about her after that. At least until tonight. There was no driving down Laurel Run Road without thinking about Willa, but running into her— Literally. That he hadn't expected.

He was stunned, knocked off balance by a barrage of feelings—regret, anger, pain—as he stared for one pounding, frozen moment into her pale, shocked face, while the storm seemed to recede around them, leaving them on a planet all by themselves. She stood there in the light, and he was speechless.

It was her, it was really her. She was a mature woman now, not a teenage girl, but all he could see in those lost, scared, hazel eyes was the girl he'd once held in his arms.

He'd thought she was perfect fourteen years ago. Delicious, sweet, innocent Willa, with her apple cheeks, sparkling river-green eyes, ribbons of wavy, gold sunshine tumbling around her shoulders. Totally oblivious to her power over every boy in town— especially the boy who lived up the road and watched her picking corn, riding her horse, swimming in the river…. Walking down the road to the river right past his granddad's farm in her itsy-bitsy bikini, carrying a damn parasol, for Christ's sake, like she'd just stepped out of a wet dream and into real life.

It'd been all in fun at first, then it had turned so wild, so hot, that they'd burned each other to the ground in the end. And what a bitter end it had been. He wasn't proud of his own behavior, but there was nothing good he could have said about hers.

He didn't have any excuses to give for the past, but neither did Willa. She had betrayed him, not the other way around.

She was still gorgeous. Drop-dead gorgeous. And she still had it—that regal air, that natural elegance, even as she stood there soaked to the bones in jeans and a work shirt that did nothing to hide the fact that her body had lost little in the translation from teenage girl to mature woman.

He felt a buzz, like some kind of electrical charge zapping through him. He hadn't felt that kind of buzz since....

No, don't even go there. He wasn't that stupid. His body might be that stupid, but not his brain. And he was no teenage idiot anymore.

"You'd better start walking." Willa whipped around—oh yeah, she was still regal—and headed for the piece of crap pickup truck in the beaten-down rock drive.

"Not so fast." He was on her in a heartbeat. Penn took her arm, stopped her in her tracks. In the past, he knew what her game had been then, or had by the end of things. She was a player, a user, a cheater. What her game was now—that's what he was going to find out.

A shocked breath escaped her at his grip.

"Get off me," she yelled at him, trying to shake off his grip.

She was surprisingly strong, but she wasn't stronger than him.

Rain lashed down. "I think we need to talk."

"I don't think so," she spat. Those green eyes rolled hot at him. "I don't know what's going on here, but this is my farm. Go back to New York City or wherever you came from, Penn Ramsey. Leave. Turn around and walk away! You're good at that!"

That shine in her eyes almost looked like tears, and that socked him hard. He shoved the feeling back. This was some kind of scam. Otto P. Ramsey had died six weeks ago while Penn was working on an overseas account, his last trip for Brown and Sons. He hadn't made it back for the service. The executor of the estate had sent him a letter and Penn had gotten in touch with him immediately on his return. He'd had the will for a few months. Otto had sent him a copy before his death, and he'd been too busy to do more than briefly argue with the old man over the phone about its details. The executor's warning had convinced him to give up fighting the residency clause. He'd spent the last month arranging his life so he could give up thirty days to fulfill the requirements in the will before coming out to West Virginia. He'd shuttered his apartment, handed in his resignation, and gotten on a plane.

There had been nothing in that document about Willa North. Hell, he had no idea what Willa North had to do with Otto at all.

"I want to know what the hell is going on here, Willa, and I want to know now. This is my farm. I'm here to claim it. If you've been squatting here, that doesn't make it—"

"I'm not squatting anywhere! This is not your farm, it's mine. I live here, and I've been living here for over a year, and if you were ever in touch with your grandfather, maybe you'd know that."

If she was trying to make him mad, she was doing a fine job. Yeah, he'd been out of touch much of the time, but not completely, and his grandfather had never mentioned Willa.

And on top of that, he was almost speechless at her gall. Or maybe he just liked being angry with her. It felt good. Better than guilt. He had plenty to be angry with her about, going back fourteen years, so it was no effort.

"When I did or didn't talk to my grandfather is none of your business. What is my business is this farm. Who else is living here? *Jared?*"

Wow, bitter, that tone in his voice. He hadn't expected that from himself. Anger, yes, but bitterness? Jared could have her.

"No. Not that it's any of your business," she told him through gritted teeth.

He barely caught her voice over the storm. Maybe they were both crazy, standing there arguing in the pouring rain. And what did she mean by that response anyway? Were she and Jared divorced then? *Not the point,* he reminded himself.

"I want you to leave," she repeated. "If you want to contest the will—" She looked terrified and determined all at once. Her hair—short, not long like he remembered it—plastered to her cheeks. Her clothing soaked to her body. "Then fine. You do that, hotshot! Talk to my attorney."

Like she had an attorney. He could tell she was

bluffing on that one by just looking at her frightened face. She was driving some beat-up piece of crap and squatting on a farm that didn't belong to her.

Maybe she really had been living with his grandfather. The old man kept secrets, he knew that. Or maybe she'd moved in after he died. She was an opportunistic excuse for a human being, he knew that, too. Maybe she thought he'd never show up to claim his property and she'd live there for free forever.

She had another think coming. He was smarter than she'd bargained for, fourteen years ago and now.

"Brilliant, Willa. Just brilliant." He dropped his hold on her arm, suddenly unable to bear the contact. "Now, why would I contest anything? The farm is mine. And if I have to go to the legal system to get you removed, I'll do it."

"It is *not* your farm."

"Are you crazy?" He was on the verge of losing his temper completely.

But she was so insistent, he could almost believe for a second she was telling the truth—or *thought* she was telling the truth—and the feeling bugged him. What if she really did have mental issues? She didn't look crazy. She looked angry and upset and scared. But what did *he* know—other than that he was going to be a hell of a lot *more* pissed off if he had to walk six miles back to town in the rain.

"The farm was left to me in the will."

It took him a full thirty seconds to realize that it

wasn't just he who had said those words, she'd said them at the same time.

Their gazes locked. He felt the shock roping between them.

"You are the crazy one," she breathed, so raw and soft he couldn't hear her. But he saw her lips move, knew what she said. She was shaking, visibly now, and white as a sheet. "Get out of here!" She yelled that. There was no missing it.

She tore off suddenly, leaving him stunned just long enough for her to get in the old Ford. The engine rattled to life and, in the light from the dash's interior, he could see her reach first one way, then the other, slamming down manual door locks.

The truck rammed backward, sliding on gravel in the drive, then reared forward. Was she *trying* to run over him? He jerked back, almost losing his balance in a dip in the gravel drive, and sidestepped out of the way.

Red taillights disappeared up the hill.

Son of a bitch. He started walking.

The house was pitch black.

"Birdie?"

Willa slammed the side door of the farmhouse as she barreled inside, turned back just as quickly to hit the bolt, then ran for the front door and then the back door, making her way by perfect memory, and bolted those, too. She wouldn't put it past Penn to come charging in here, since he seemed to think he owned the place.

"Birdie!" she yelled again.

She heard the telltale sound of Flash's doggy nails padding through the house toward her. A second later, the hound—part basset, part whatever—was pawing at her legs, then dropping down to go check his food dish.

The old house creaked in the wind outside. Had to be a tree down somewhere. Electricity was the first to go out here. Phones next. She fumbled for a phone, checked the line. Dead, as expected.

Cell service was only a fantasy in the country, so the isolation was quick and complete.

If Penn came stomping up here, she'd have no way to call for help. She stood there in the old house, a shiver crawling up her spine.

Creepy, that's what this house was sometimes in the dark, in the storm, during lonely nights. Yet she loved it, every crumbling inch of its Gothic architecture. She'd moved in the week of the Haven earthquake, and sometimes the town's collective, overly active imagination about the consequences of that so-called "perfect storm" of low pressure, dense moisture, and geologic instability, niggled at her mind.

She'd seen the bursts of red lights right here on the farm, the same mysterious lights that had been talked about in town and on cable news, when a paranormal detective had been interviewed. Foundational movement for oncoming paranormal activity, the spokesperson for PAI, the Paranormal Activity Institute, had claimed. Nonsense, of course.

Most people had been scared that night, but for some reason, Willa had felt folded in, protected. Nothing on the farm had been damaged. The house, with all its aged faults, had held its ground, while the building in town where she and Birdie had rented an apartment, had crumbled. She had come to this house at just the right time, and the house had saved her. She knew that was fanciful dreaming, not anything supernatural, though. And those moments when she got a little creeped out? That was just the insidious whispers in town about strange happenings getting to her…and the dark, sometimes lonely nights.

The house breathed history, history she didn't have on her own, and to her, it also breathed the future. It was hers! Penn and his cousins had been treated fairly in the will. They had nothing to complain about.

Where had any of them been during Otto Ramsey's dying days?

Who had cared for him out of love, not money?

Not a one of his grandchildren. And she had loved the old man, despite his sins. He had been like her own grandfather, the one she'd never had in her own, torn-up, far-flung, dysfunctional family.

She called Birdie again, headed through the dark house for the kitchen, Flash at her heels. Maybe Birdie was sleeping. She needed a flashlight. And she didn't even want to think about Penn Ramsey, much less how much trouble she was going to be in if she had to come up with the cash to fight for what she'd been given. She didn't want to think about how awful it had felt right down to her bones to see him, either. What he'd said about the house being left to him in the will…

Total crap.

Maybe he had an old will. Otto Ramsey had written a new one, and left the farm to her. He'd left investment money to his niece Jess, and the same to Penn. Another old family property had gone to his other grandson, Marcus, who'd moved into a house out there years ago and didn't care about Limberlost any more than Penn and Jess ever had.

What if she was the one with an outdated will, and Penn had a newer one? No, no, she was so not going to think that way. She couldn't believe Otto Ramsey would do that to her.

Not after what had happened. Not after how he'd promised her to make up for it.

She owned this farm. She and Birdie. He'd promised it to Birdie as much as he'd promised it to her. He'd doted on the girl. He wouldn't do this to Birdie.

Willa reached the kitchen, called Birdie and held carefully still, listening to the old house breathe. Birdie was a light sleeper. Surely she would wake up as she'd called her. But…

No patter of little socked feet. No, *"I'm in here, Mama."* She felt an anxious tightening in her stomach. What if…?

She dropped the pickup keys on the scarred farmhouse table in the kitchen where she now stood. She pulled open a drawer where another flashlight was kept, then headed for the stairs, ordering herself not to panic. Birdie wouldn't have gone anywhere....

Would she? She'd told her to stay put. Willa'd looked out the window a few hours ago, seen through the leaf-barren trees in the dusky light that cows were in the road below. By the time she'd rounded up all but the one recalcitrant calf and gotten the fence fixed, it'd been long past dark.

She'd left Birdie watching TV. Birdie always got scared when the lights went out. Storms scared her, too. Birdie was like her. Or like she had been, once: timid, innocent, often shy. She hoped her daughter wouldn't have to toughen up the way she had. She wanted so much for Birdie, so much more than she'd had.

Willa pushed down the lump that swelled in her throat and took the stairs in bounds. The house was filled with old, original wood paneling that made dark corners everywhere in the dead of night, though it could be beautiful by day. The flashlight bounced gold globes of light as she raced up, Flash right behind her. The wall was lined with old photographs, some in sepia, some in black-and-white. It was a wall of eyes, and sometimes she thought it was the creepiest part of the farmhouse.

Birdie's room was the first one to the right. Bed,

empty. She whirled, ran to her own room to see if Birdie had gone in there.

"Birdie!"

Her bed—empty, too.

She called her daughter's name again. Flash barked, as if picking up on her distress. No response. *Dammit, dammit, dammit!* And she'd been down there in the road, worrying about a calf.

Willa flew back down the hall, down the stairs, past all those eyes, back into the front parlor, nearly tripping over Flash in the process. No Birdie.

She could hear the boom of her heart.

Birdie's favorite stuffed horse lay at the foot of the antique rocker in one corner. Interlocking blocks scattered across the green and blue-rag area rug between the stone fireplace and the old, brown suede sofa. Crayon drawings and worn-down colors occupied an old camp box that served as a coffee table.

Panic shifted to full throttle.

What if Birdie had gone outside to look for her—fallen down, gotten hurt? Maybe she was even unconscious. Dead in a ditch. Her mother's mind leaped to every worst-case scenario. She wanted to call the police, but surely that was silly. She hadn't even looked outside yet.

And the phone was dead anyway.

She could drive out for help; but what if Birdie came back? She had to be here for Birdie. She had to find Birdie. Alone, in the storm. *Oh, God.* She ran for the door.

A sudden, heavy pounding on the front door nearly had her jumping out of her skin. She stopped short. Penn. She'd totally forgotten about Penn.

"Willa! Open up!"

She didn't want to talk to Penn. She didn't want to see Penn. No way was she opening that door. There was no pretending she was all big and bad, when she was in a total panic.

Tears, absolutely unallowable, pathetic, weak tears burst right down her cheeks. She swiped at them roughly. *Birdie. She had to think about Birdie.*

She forced her feet to eat up the last few steps, flung the door wide.

"Willa—"

"My daughter's missing," she interrupted him.

"What?"

"My daughter is missing! I'm afraid she went outside. I'm afraid she went looking for me. I'm afraid..."

Tears, clogging her throat. She didn't want Penn Ramsey's help. She didn't want *anyone's* help, but least of all his. And he was staring at her like she was out of her mind.

Which, of course, she was.

She pushed past him. Screw him. Stupid of her to think he'd help.

Powerful arms hauled her back. Back against a

chest so hard, so warm, so… Oh God! So capable—
so what she needed right now. A strong, capable man,
when she was in a panic.

What was wrong with her? A man was the last
thing she wanted ever again, for the rest of her life.
Stop falling apart, she ordered herself.

He turned her in his arms and he was right there,
a breath away. Her arms were mashed to his chest,
the flashlight pointed upward, illuminating the cut of
his jaw, the straight line of his nose, the disturbing
intensity of his eyes.

Her pulse thumped off the charts.

"Do you have another flashlight?" he demanded.

She shook—fear, or something else, she had no
idea. Her brain had up and quit. *Flashlight. He asked
for a flashlight.* He was going to help her find Birdie.
And she was going to force herself to let him,
because Birdie was more important than her pride or
her self-sufficiency or even this house.

"I—yes." She ran to the kitchen, flung the drawer
open so hard it fell on the floor. She dropped to her
knees, using the flashlight to find the flashlight, scattering fallen kitchen tools and notepads and nonsense
out of her way.

She bounded back to her feet and nearly barreled
right into Penn. He took the other flashlight out of
her trembling hand. She felt the warmth of his fingers
brush hers, electric.

Scary.

She felt tears on her cheeks again.

"Willa." His voice, searingly soft now, froze her to the worn, hardwood floor. "It's going to be okay. We'll find her."

She swallowed hard, nodded. "Of course." She had to find Birdie. *Had* to. And would. No other outcome was tolerable.

But she didn't believe everything was going to be okay. Not so long as he stayed.

Chapter 3

They were both already soaked to the skin, and
going back out into this wild storm was only going
to make things worse. But there was no other choice.
A dog bounded up behind her, barking.

"Get a jacket, Willa."

She looked at him blankly, then turned, told the
dog to hush and opened a closet near the front door
to grab a rain slicker. She put it on, pulling the hood
over her head, and moved past him to the door that
was still standing open wide, the dog trotting right
after her. She avoided meeting Penn's eyes. She
looked small in the oversize slicker. The short, wispy
cut of her hair revealed every delicate line of her

features, features that looked fragile now, like glass ready to shatter.

But she was tougher than she looked, he knew that.

He followed her out onto the wide, covered farmhouse porch. Old rocking chairs with peeling paint lined up in front of the house, the way they always had. A porch swing's chains rattled in the wind at the far end.

"How old is your daughter?"

"She's four."

Four. God. This wild night was no place for a four-year-old child. No wonder Willa looked like she was about to go crazy.

"You're positive she's not in the house?"

"Of course I'm positive she's not in the house!"

"Where's the other one?" The other one that should be almost fourteen now.

"What other one?" she asked impatiently. Then… She now met his eyes. "There is no other one."

She walked away from him.

"Birdie!" she shouted, her voice hopelessly lost in the wind and rain.

There is *no other one.* He shouldn't even want to explore that, and now wasn't the time to find out what had happened to the baby Willa had been carrying the day he'd walked away. It hadn't been his baby, anyway. And this wasn't the time to think about that betrayal, either.

He hurried after Willa and the stumpy-legged mutt that kept pace with her. She'd asked for his help, but he was damn sure she didn't really want it. She loved her daughter—that was clear, too.

Loved her enough to ask him for help.

He caught up with her at the bottom of the porch steps, reached for her arm to stop her.

"It's important right now not to race off in a hundred directions," he said grimly. "Does she have any favorite places on the farm? Hiding spots? We'll search there and the barn, then we go back and call the police if we don't find her."

"The phones are out already."

"Then we go for help in your truck. Or one of us goes for help while the other one stays here," he added, seeing the resistance on her face before she even opened her mouth. She didn't want to leave Birdie alone, even if they didn't know where the child was.

But it was just as obvious that they couldn't search four hundred acres by themselves. The farm was massive and partly wild. Otto had abandoned any real farming years ago, and much of the land had grown up over time, turned back into woods. In the old days, Otto's father before him had had all kinds of money, but not from farming. There was oil and gas under this farm, and at the turn of the last century, there'd been drilling everywhere. Most of those wells had been abandoned decades ago, leaving nothing but rusted well sheds and crumbling derricks, not to mention pipes running everywhere, some of them sticking out of the ground or jaggedly cut off.

There were plenty of ways for a child to run into trouble or to get hurt rambling around in the dark while panicked. Plenty of ways for Willa to get hurt, too.

He wondered what kind of name Birdie was, but he didn't ask. Willa charged off and he kept up with her. In the bouncing flashlight beam, he spied the old herb garden to the side of the house, with its paving stone paths and geometric design, the huge stone sundial in the center. And he saw something new in the shadows beyond it.

Wooden playground equipment. *What the hell?*

Maybe she had been living at Limberlost for a year, after all. Eighty-two-year-old Otto Ramsey hadn't put in a slide and swings for himself.

There was a barn on the hill and another below, in the meadow. As far as he was concerned, if they didn't find her up here, there was no sense heading farther afield before getting help. But he'd have to convince Willa of that.

The wind ripped back Willa's hood, baring her head as she ran toward the barn. He chased after her, helped her with the heavy wooden latch on the barn door. Inside, their flashlights swerved and crossed. She called Birdie's name. The barn smelled earthy and like home, and he was stunned for a harsh instant. There were horse stalls up and down the barn, but only one horse poked its ebony head over a stall door.

Willa raced between the stalls, looking into every

one. She whirled at the end of the barn, faced him. Raw emotion hit him again, this time with the appalling urge to take her into arms and promise her he'd find Birdie.

He shoved the thought away as he saw the steel under her painful fear.

"Where now?" he asked.

"She has a treehouse. That's all I can think."

"Let's go."

They left the barn. He latched the door while she tore ahead. He followed the erratic bounce of her flashlight beam in the wind and rain.

Willa climbed the wooden steps nailed to a huge cherry tree before he even got there, and nearly fell down into his arms as she barreled back down.

"She's not there!" Her eyes flashed a near-hysteria that she was clearly working hard to control.

"Get me the keys to your truck."

She didn't hesitate. He raced after her toward the house, but she was back in the doorway with a set of keys before he reached it.

"Please." Her eyes shone bright in the dark. "Please get help." She was begging, and clearly past caring who was helping her.

She stood in the door, the light from her flashlight spilling at her feet. The truck was parked at the side of the house. He jumped in, gunned the engine to life, and started to back up when he realized abruptly what felt so strange about the way the vehicle sat.

He got out, slammed the door, and flashed his light down at the tires.

The rear passenger-side tire was flat.

His blood froze in his veins. He knelt down and studied the tire in the light. He couldn't see any reason for it to be flat, though the rubber was thinning and hadn't worn well. No obvious puncture, or at least not one he could see in this light. He went for the spare, soaked beyond belief at this point, and stood back, stomach hitting the ground when he pulled it out.

The spare was flat.

He'd never seen so many things go wrong in unison in his whole life—from the failed brakes on the Land Rover right up to Willa's tires. Maybe that text message he'd gotten this morning had been from the Universe.

But if he hadn't come to Haven tonight...

Willa would be alone right now. And no matter how he felt about her and the past, the thought of her being alone in these circumstances brought out every protective instinct in his body.

Stupid and incomprehensible and flat-out crazy as that was.

Penn turned, headed for the house, dreading giving her the news. Willa's daughter was out there, and no matter what had happened in the past or how Willa had hurt him, or even what kind of mess they had in front of them over the will, there was a lost little girl, and that was all that mattered right now.

Willa yanked the door wide before he reached it. He could see the same dread in his gut on her face before he opened his mouth.

"The truck's got a flat and the spare's flat, too," he told her.

"I just drove the truck!" She didn't want to believe him. In fact, she pushed past him as if she thought he was lying.

He followed her back out into the rain. She ran to the truck, dropped to her knees in front of the tire, then was back up, wheeling to find the spare where he'd left it on the ground.

She looked up at him then.

Her face was so stricken, so pale in the shine of his flashlight, he couldn't tell the difference between tears and raindrops on her cheeks; but he knew it was a combination of both that he saw.

"Did you do this?" she yelled at him over the storm.

"What?"

"What is going on? Did you flatten the tires?"

"Are you crazy?"

"I'm sorry." She deflated, pressed shaking fingers to her mouth. She turned away, stared desperately out into the storm-dark woods.

He wanted to blame her for that bit of insanity, but he knew she was out of her mind with worry. Whatever else he didn't believe about Willa, what he did believe was her love for her daughter. He didn't know why it stunned him so. Even animals had mothering instincts. Willa didn't have to be a perfect person to love her child.

Still, it rocked the cold, ugly image he had made up in his mind about Willa's character.

"I have to find her," she shouted now, wildly.

"Not alone."

She stared at him for a long, awful moment. She was terrified, that was clear, and not just of the storm and her lost daughter.

Willa was terrified of *him.*

That rocked the cold, ugly image, too. She was vulnerable.

"I *am* alone," she said with an achy honesty that seared him even deeper.

Again, he wanted to know what had happened to Jared. Why Willa would have been living with Otto. How she came to be alone.

"Not tonight," he said. "You're not alone tonight."

Obviously, she wasn't thinking clearly, though maybe if she wasn't scared of him, a man she'd once betrayed, a man she hadn't seen in fourteen years, she would be certifiable for sure.

"And you can't just go charging out there," he went on. "I know there's a map of the property here somewhere. We'll get extra batteries and we'll organize our own grid search. It's important that you don't get lost as well. Birdie needs you."

He saw her throat move in the wild darkness.

"I'm scared," she finally said. "I don't understand

what's happening, but something is really wrong. I'm scared!"

And he knew she hadn't wanted to admit that out loud, knew she regretted it right away. She hated being vulnerable, hated it and wanted to hide it, and she couldn't. She was too scared, teetering on full-blown panic.

And that's why he didn't tell her that he was scared, too. Something *was* wrong. This entire series of events was bizarre.

The spring wind whipped higher, colder, suddenly, and something hard struck his head, his arms. The hound yelped, hit.

Hail.

Huge, golf ball-sized hail. The kind of hail that could kill a person.

"Run!" he yelled, grabbing Willa's arm, dragging her in the opposite direction of where he knew she wanted to go.

Penn gave her no choice, forced her into a dead run toward the house, and Willa was terrified her skull was going to be split in two by the hail at any second. And what good would she do Birdie then?

They reached the house and he yanked open the door. Willa ran inside, Flash whimpering at her heels, and she pivoted back to see Penn's dark figure fill the doorway behind her.

The door shut, blocking the storm and the terrible

night, leaving her wet and shaking and scared as he turned around.

"What about Birdie?" she half sobbed, and caught herself.

She was looking to him, Penn, to tell her what to do now. She was so far gone, it was ridiculous. How could so many things go wrong at once?

Penn's gaze riveted beyond her.

"Willa—" he started.

She felt a prickle at the nape of her neck.

"Mommy."

The scream that had been clawing its way up Willa's throat came all the way out.

She dropped her flashlight and swung wildly. There Birdie stood, in her favorite Pooh Bear jammies. Her big hazel eyes gazed up at Willa, so big, so bright, without her glasses. Emotion smashed into Willa. She didn't remember moving her feet across the short distance that separated them. She was just there, reaching for her daughter.

"Birdie, Birdie, Birdie." She sobbed her daughter's name over and over as she clutched her against her chest, dropping down, nearly falling crazily backward as she held her.

Birdie lifted her small face to her, her eyes wide and scared. Willa was scaring Birdie. She had to pull herself together.

"I was worried about you, sweetie. I couldn't find you."

"I was sleeping."

"You weren't in your bed!"

"I was in *your* bed, Mama. I was scared of the storm."

Birdie hadn't been in *her* bed! She'd checked! But right now she didn't care, it was a senseless point. She couldn't resist tugging Birdie tightly against her one more time. Wherever she *had* been, she was here now. In her arms.

"You're wet, Mama," she mumbled into Willa's chest, wriggling in her mother's arms.

"I know. I'm sorry." She was soaked and she didn't care. But she didn't need to soak Birdie, too. She forced herself to let Birdie draw back.

Emotion still shot her pulse off the scale. Birdie was alive, in her arms. She wanted to just sit down and cry and hold her precious daughter.

"Who's that man, Mama?"

Willa scrambled to her feet, controlling the sudden, silly—she knew it was silly—this urge to push Birdie behind her to keep her safe. As if she needed to protect her from Penn. Penn had been helping her to search for Birdie.

But he was also the one who was here to threaten the very foundation of her and Birdie's lives, take this farm away from them.

Penn's gaze, stark in the shadows cast by the flashlight he held directed low, struck her tightly, intensely. Even from several feet away, she felt as if he loomed over her, making her feel short despite her five feet, seven inches. He was… *Big* was the only word that came to mind.

Yeah. Big and bad. Good-looking and arrogant. A city slicker here to smash her like a bug beneath his steely boot.

That was difficult to remember when she was also grateful to him. And way too emotional.

Chapter 4

"She's okay. Birdie's okay." Tears, rolling. Willa could feel them hot on her cold cheeks. Dammit. Reaction was setting in, and all the fear and tension was coming out in tears now. She swiped hard at her cheeks. Now was the time to get back in control. "Maybe I panicked. I didn't see her anywhere."

She might have felt silly, but she was still too relieved to have Birdie back to worry about how strange it was that she hadn't been able to find her right there in the house. It was almost as if she'd disappeared and reappeared. Magically.

Penn shook his head. "Forget it. I'm just glad she's all right. That's all that matters."

Willa swallowed hard. "Yeah." Even now, the thought of Birdie being out there in that storm alone, instead of right here… It was a terrifying image that still had her shaking. If there was any magic going on, it was a bad magic, that was for sure. Not that she believed in such things.

Then it registered in her mind…that Penn had nowhere to go.

What was she going to do with him now? It was late. His brakes were out. She had a flat tire. The storm was raging outside. There was no way to call anyone, and they were miles from town.

With everything that had happened so quickly and her worries about Birdie, she hadn't even thought about what was going to happen next. She'd been angrily ready to walk away from him on the road after he'd struck her with his car and claimed this farm was his.

But now…

He'd done everything to help her when she'd needed it, hadn't he?

Her heart pounded. She took a step, bent down to retrieve the flashlight she'd dropped, and gave it to Birdie.

Magic. She wouldn't mind having some for real.

"Why don't you go in the kitchen, sweetie?" she said. "See if you can find the cocoa and marshmallows. I'll fix you a cup of hot chocolate before you go back to bed."

Luckily, she had a gas stove and gas heat throughout the house, or they'd be freezing tonight. She hadn't remembered to bring in more logs for the fireplace, and with the way the wind was whipping, she doubted the tarp cover had stayed on the woodpile.

And maybe she didn't want to think about her real problem.

"Who's that man, Mama?"

She didn't want to answer that question, even if the answer was simple. Something about introducing Penn to her daughter bothered her. As if introducing him to Birdie was going to make him part of her life. She didn't want him to be part of her life, or Birdie's. And she was being silly again.

Maybe.

But it seemed as if, ever since he'd arrived at Limberlost, events had spiraled to entwine him more and more in her life, at least temporarily. They'd gone from an unfortunate encounter on the road to…her being stuck with him, and indebted just enough, that tossing him out in the storm was no longer possible.

"His name is Penn. He's…an old friend." Close enough.

Explaining that he was Otto's grandson seemed like more information than Birdie needed at the moment. Or maybe she just didn't like knowing that Birdie would be even more interested in him if she knew that. Birdie had loved Otto, and she was a curious little girl about everything.

"Go on, Birdie," she prodded firmly. "I'll be there

in a minute. You go find the cocoa and marshmallows for me."

Birdie took the flashlight and skipped off to the kitchen. Literally skipped. She certainly had plenty of energy. Willa felt drained. She yanked off the rain slicker and laid it over the back of a rocking chair in the parlor, giving herself a bit of distance.

She looked back at Penn. He still stood in front of the door, dripping onto the scarred hardwood floor. He exuded the same infuriatingly cool self-confidence he always had. She'd been attracted to that once. Now it scared her more than she wanted to admit.

"You okay?" he asked.

"Of course. I'm fine."

He continued to regard her with those laser-intense eyes of his, as if he could read her mind and knew she was lying.

The past seemed to pulsate between them. It was the elephant in the room that neither one wanted to talk about, but that was difficult to ignore.

"Thank you for helping me." She felt as if she had to force each word out of her mouth with a cattle prod. And it sounded that way. Ungrateful. Insincere.

"You're welcome."

This conversation was killing her.

"You can stay here tonight," she said. "There's no other choice."

Penn's gaze didn't waver. "Of course I can stay here. It's my house."

Was he *trying* to make her head blow up? She refused to pick up the bait—and now she wasn't the least bit sorry if she'd sounded ungrateful.

"I'm not discussing the will." She wondered what he wanted with this old house anyway. If he had it, he'd just sell the farm and go back to wherever he came from with the money.

Did he want money that badly? He'd made a success of himself in the city, she knew that much from Otto. And the farm wasn't worth a tiny percent of the money Otto had left his grandchildren.

Years ago, in the oil and gas boom, Limberlost had made a pretty penny for the Ramseys. Those days were long gone, but Otto had been a smart investor, and his grandchildren had nothing to complain about.

"I'm sure you remember where your grandfather's bedroom is, and I'm sure you'll feel free to help yourself to anything you find in there."

No need to play hostess when he was treating her like a squatter. Anger was rather freeing, she decided. She liked it.

She found Birdie in the kitchen playing with Mop, their gray tabby, who had crawled out from wherever she'd been hiding to chase the flashlight beam across the floor. Apparently, her daughter had gotten distracted on her way to find the cocoa and marshmallows.

Willa took matches from a drawer and lit the big, handmade, jarred, vanilla-brandy-scented candle, then scooped up the mess from the drawer she'd pulled out earlier, just as Mop skidded through it after the flashlight beam, scattering papers and pens and utensils to the corners of the room. She'd just started selling her handmade candles, soaps and knitting patterns online, in addition to at a consignment shop in town, and there went all her receipts for the month. Not that she should be jamming receipts into an already overstuffed drawer.

She had way too much going on, that was a fact.

"Birdie! Could you not shine it here until I get this picked up?"

"Sorry, Mommy."

Willa felt a little niggle of guilt for the sharp edge to her voice. She was upset with Penn…and herself. Not Birdie.

She got the drawer with all her receipts put back together, and found some votive holders and more candles. The old kitchen flickered with light and filled with the vanilla-brandy scent of the candles. Birdie giggled as Mop again ran across the floor after her dancing flashlight.

This evening could be a whole lot worse. Birdie could have been missing in the storm.

It could be a whole lot better, too; but she was going to have to work on her attitude, since she couldn't do anything about what was wrong with this evening. Not tonight, at least.

"Okay, now *really* get out the cocoa and marshmallows, Birdie. I'll be right back." She couldn't stand her wet clothes another minute.

Willa grabbed the matches again and hurried out of the kitchen and up the stairs—in the pitch dark, since she'd left the flashlight with Birdie. She found her way by habit to her bedroom and shut the door. The storm raged outside still, the wind creaking around the sides of the old farmhouse. The hail seemed to have dissipated, since she wasn't hearing the hard knocks against the tin roof anymore.

Dragging a match against the side of the box, she lit the room enough to find the candle on her dresser. There was no dearth of candles, though she usually felt guilty for burning them. She needed to sell them, not use them.

Her pulse thunked hard as she looked into the mirror over the antique Queen Anne dresser. Her hair was a wild mess, even short as it was only coming to below her chin. It was thick, starting to frizz up damply, and she wished she'd let it grow instead of cutting it to just below her chin the last time she'd had her hair done, so she could have tied it back to get it under control.

She wore no makeup and her skin glowed pale in the flickering light. She was tired and almost light-headed, and she would have loved nothing more than to curl up in bed and maybe cry some more, alone.

But Birdie was downstairs—and this night wasn't over yet, not by a long shot.

Toughen up, she told herself. She'd indulged in enough meltdowns for one evening. She was going to have to go back downstairs, emotionally exhausted or not.

She tugged open the top drawer and pulled out the first thing she found, a fresh pair of jeans, and in the next drawer down, a thick, oversize sweatshirt. She changed clothes quickly, tossing the wet things on the floor.

Turning, her glance landed, froze, on the big spool bed in the middle of the room. The quilt was an old-fashioned wedding ring pattern in greens and blues, almost threadbare in places, but Willa loved it along with the antiquey atmosphere of the furnishings. She'd changed very little about the room since she'd moved into it.

How had she missed Birdie on the bed earlier? She felt a tingle in the pit of her stomach. She didn't understand, but she had enough trouble without worrying about how she'd been such a panicked ninny. She had Birdie back, that was the important thing.

The hall was dark, the candle from her room not casting its light far. She couldn't see down the hall to the room that had been Otto's. None of the family had come to clean out his personal possessions, and in her mind, she hadn't had the heart or the right.

She'd expected his granddaughter, Jess, to come take care of it, but Jess kept saying she was busy. She'd told Willa the last time they'd talked to give his clothes away. There wasn't much of any value in the house, other than the antiques, and even they weren't fine quality for the most part—more sentimental than valuable on an objective basis—and other than specific items that had been listed in the will for his grandchildren out of the house, the bulk of the home's possessions had been left to Willa with the farm. Even so, she'd told Jess she could take anything she wanted.

Otto's grandchildren weren't the most sentimental bunch, as far as she could see. Willa, on the other hand, loved everything in the house. She didn't have much in the way of family history and mementos of her own. She'd adopted Otto, the way he'd adopted her and Birdie.

She'd be damned if Penn was going to breeze into town and take it all away from her. Otto had known his grandchildren didn't care about the house and the history and the old things. But Willa had, and he'd known that, too.

In the morning, hopefully there'd be some way to get Penn out of here. Then she'd call an attorney and scrounge up the money somewhere, to figure out what was going on and to protect what Otto had promised her.

She went down the dark stairs. Laughter and voices carried from the kitchen. One high, excited, one low, competent.

Her feet moved faster, and as she came around the

corner of the stairs and reached the open doorway into the kitchen, light from the candles and the stove hit her.

Penn was standing at the cooktop, the gas lit, spooning cocoa into a pot. Birdie had the aluminum and Formica stool pulled up the way she liked to do, and was perched on the edge of it, gazing up at their guest, with big, glowing eyes. She was holding on to Mop, who didn't want to be held. She wrestled with the squirming cat, dropping her as Willa walked in.

Alarm bells sounded in her veins at the too-domestic little scene, and she could feel her heart banging against the wall of her chest. She saw Penn reaching for a drawer to the right of the stove.

"That drawer doesn't work," Birdie told him. She twisted around to open the drawer on the other side of where she sat, then handed him a ladle to stir the hot chocolate as he poured the milk in.

Birdie spotted Willa. "Mommy, he's Mr. Otto's grandson!" she announced, as if this might be news to Willa. "And he said you used to be his girlfriend!"

Okay, that was enough.

"What do you think you're doing?" Willa demanded.

Penn turned, finally, from the stove. The candle-light cast gentle shadows and light that softened the handsome planes and angles of his face. He was unbelievably good-looking, and that she had to notice that, even when she was seriously thinking about throttling him, scared the crap out of her. He'd put on a comfortably worn, flannel work shirt that had been his grandfather's, and he looked shockingly at home making hot chocolate in her kitchen.

"Making hot chocolate," he said quietly. "You want some?"

Willa resisted the urge to stomp her foot.

"You don't get to just come in here and act like you're at home," she said angrily—too angrily. For a hot instant, she forgot about Birdie sitting there listening. "I'll make my own daughter's hot chocolate. Then we're going upstairs to bed. And I suggest you do the same. You'll be up early, hiking out of here if you have to!"

"That's not very nice, Mommy," Birdie piped in.

"Go on upstairs, Birdie. Wait for me in my room. You can sleep in there with me tonight. I'll bring you your hot chocolate in a minute, when I come up." She strode to the stove and all but pushed Penn out of the way. He stepped aside casually, and not very far. "I've had it up to here with tonight. The cows getting loose. *You* nearly running over me." She shot a dagger look at Penn, then looked back to stir the hot chocolate like there was no tomorrow. "Birdie missing. The electricity and phones going out. The flat tires. The hail." *Now he was telling Birdie they used to go out.* She was on a roll, and at the moment she was pretty sure everything was Penn's fault, somehow. "And you are pushing it," she said to Penn without looking at him.

Birdie had not gotten off her stool.

"You're not going to make him leave, are you, Mommy? Don't be mad!"

Willa blew out a frustrated breath, tried to rein in her temper. If she was going to tell Penn off, she shouldn't be doing it in front of Birdie. "He has to leave tomorrow, sweetie. But not tonight."

She refused to look at him. Penn hadn't budged a step out of the kitchen, either. No doubt, he felt he had full run of the place and he wasn't too concerned about whether he was welcome or not.

"Because he can't leave." Birdie tugged on Willa's sleeve. "He can't leave. The house wants him here!"

Willa turned. "What? The house doesn't want anything, Birdie. Don't be silly."

It seemed as if the storm hushed and the house went dead still. Willa could hear her pulse rush in her ears. *This is ridiculous,* she had the sense to think to herself, and yet, she could feel the hair rising on the back of her neck.

This was all she needed to top off her evening. Some kind of woo-woo nonsense from a four-year-old. Nights with no electricity weren't good times to tell creepy stories, and Birdie always had a big imagination. Maybe they spent too much time alone here on the farm.

"Yes, it does!" Birdie insisted. "The house wants everybody to stay right here!"

"Why?" As if the house was capable of wanting

anything. Even for flight-of-fancy Birdie, that idea was a little extreme. Children, the PAI spokesperson had said, were more susceptible to paranormal activity because their young minds were so open—and every once in a while Birdie made such odd remarks, Willa wondered if that was true. And then she'd wonder what was wrong with her, because that was a notion that depended on there actually being something paranormal for Birdie to be susceptible to.

The whole thing was ridiculous, just like the lingering feeling she'd had for so long that the house was here to protect her. Good magic, bad magic—she didn't believe in any of it.

"I don't know why the house wants us here." Birdie shrugged. "Maybe it likes us."

"Go upstairs, Birdie," Willa repeated. *The house liked them. Sure.*

Wind kicked up outside the old farmhouse. Birdie got off the stool.

"Can I take Mop?"

"Yes. If you can catch her. And don't forget Berry Bear." If Birdie didn't have her bear, they'd never get a good night's sleep.

Birdie danced the flashlight on the floor and managed to entice the cat to follow her out. *Well, at least that would keep her busy.*

Willa spun on Penn. "Did you put that in her head?"

"Put what in her head?"

"That idea about the house. Did you tell her the

house wanted you here?" *What a manipulator he was.* "You told her plenty else!"

"She asked how we knew each other."

He was calm, cool, collected. Very annoying. Nothing she said seemed to irritate him, while everything he said irritated her.

"Just because she asks questions, it doesn't mean you have to answer them."

"Why are you so angry, Willa?" He stood there, leaning against her counter, his deep, inscrutable eyes steady on her.

She looked away. The hot chocolate was ready, thank goodness. She switched off the burner and reached for a mug in the cabinet. The hand she used to pick up the pot shook.

"I don't have to answer questions either," she told him. "We're in an unfortunate situation. Let's not make it worse."

"I think you're making things worse all by yourself, Willa. You don't need my help."

She set the pot down and looked at him. He *was* trying to make her head blow up, she was sure of it now. He was calm as you please, but he was deliberately provoking her. He was enjoying this situation—as she was not.

"At least I'm being honest," she blurted hotly. "I'm not pretending, the way you are."

"Oh, I think you're pretending, Willa." He cocked his head, crossed his arms.

God, he was so arrogant.

And he wasn't done.

"You're not angry with me. You're just scared. And not because you think I'm going to take your house. You're pretending you can't stand me, but that's not the way you feel at all, is it?"

Chapter 5

Oh, Willa was mad now. As if she hadn't already been mad. She'd been angry since she'd looked him in the face down on the road and realized who he was.

But he was still right. She was off-the-charts-upset with him being there, and it wasn't because she hated him.

And maybe, Penn thought, he'd lost his mind a little bit to be enjoying that realization, but there it was. Willa had destroyed what they'd had, and whatever her life had been since then, it hadn't been easy, he could see that.

She refused to look at him. She leaned across the counter and started blowing out candles, her movements jerky and quick. She took the last candle, still lit, and the mug of hot chocolate.

"Get out of my way," she hissed.

She sounded angry still. Angrier, in fact. But that was the fear; and suddenly, he couldn't say another word to torment her. She wasn't the only one pretending about their feelings here.

He was pretending, too. And he wasn't sure for how long. Truthfully, she'd tiptoed through his mind for years, and even more painfully truthful, a little secret part of him had wanted to see her again. Out of curiosity or insanity, he wasn't sure. Maybe he'd even thought seeing her again would help him wipe her out of his mind forever. He hadn't even realized he wanted to see her until now.

"We need to talk," he said.

"Our lawyers can talk."

He shook his head. "Willa, let's figure this out. In the morning, I'll get my things out of the Land Rover. I've got a copy of the will. You show me your copy and we'll—"

What he was saying made sense, but she wasn't hearing him.

"I'm exhausted," she said, almost desperately. "Please let me go to bed."

It was the "please" that did him in. He knew that word came hard for her right now—said to him—and he couldn't push her anymore, at least not tonight. There was always tomorrow. Before he left, he'd get her to show him her copy of the will. There had to be some way to make sense of this mess.

He stepped out of her way.

She walked out of the room with Birdie's mug of hot chocolate and the last candle. He still had one of the flashlights. He waited for her to make her way up the stairs.

He held his flashlight without turning it on, standing in the dark room, listening to the creaking wind, the rattling house. It had been years since he'd been back to Limberlost for even a brief visit. Contrary to Willa's words, he'd kept in touch with his grandfather; but visits to Haven had been few and far between. Otto had come to New York once, and stayed at Penn's apartment in the city. He'd never been to New York City before, and Penn had taken off work to show him around. Otto had complained about the noise and the crowds and the taxis. He couldn't have been a more cantankerous and unpleasant house guest, and Penn had been relieved when he'd put him back on the plane at JFK. Awkward and dutiful phone calls every couple of months were a lot easier than spending time with that old coot, that was for sure.

Penn had nothing to be proud of about his relationship with his grandfather; as he stood there in the house where Otto had died, he knew that on some level, Willa was right about that.

Coming home included a lot more uncomfortable

realizations than he'd expected—not the least of which being that he wanted to talk to Willa, and not just about the will.

He snapped on the flashlight and headed for the stairs. He was losing his mind, now he was certain of it. He shouldn't feel sorry for Willa, and he shouldn't feel anything else, either. He shouldn't trust her or believe she was doing anything but running some kind of scam.

But he was having a real hard time thinking about anything other than what it had felt like, briefly, to hold her when she'd barreled into him earlier. How soft she'd felt, how he'd once had the right to touch her whenever he wanted, and how she'd once welcomed him rather than freezing in his arms.

He passed the shut door to Willa's room. Standing there in a lull of the wind, he could hear the soft sound of her daughter's voice, hear Willa telling her to go to sleep.

Where was Birdie's father? What had happened to turn Willa into such a fierce fighter? How had she come to live in Otto's house?

A hundred questions clawed at his mind, and he wondered if he had the answers, if they would satisfy him. Or if he'd only have more questions.

Willa cuddled Birdie close to her body under the covers, grateful finally for the steady, even breaths that told her Birdie slept. All the meaning in her life was right here, in this bed, in her arms, and she was all Birdie had, too. Life had been difficult for them both, after Jared's death. Birdie had been two and a half, old enough to wander around their little house on her toddler legs, crying "Da-Da" for months. She didn't even remember her daddy now, except from pictures Willa had given her.

There had been a time when Jared had saved Willa's life, but things had gone downhill from there. She didn't miss him, though she told Birdie she did. She lied about a lot of things that she convinced herself were necessary. Here was the story—stick to it, and get on with life. As much as lies hurt, the truth hurt more in some cases.

She could have told Penn the truth a long time ago, but he wouldn't have liked it. He'd just know how stupid she'd been, when all she really wanted was to forget it. She had her pride, and that was something. And maybe there was a part of her that still did think it was her fault.

She'd made her decisions, she'd told her stories. She'd had a miscarriage two and a half months after she'd married Jared, and she'd stuck with him out of gratitude, even when he started drinking, stopped working and ran her down all the time. He'd been her savior at one time, and maybe she'd thought she could save him. She couldn't. He'd killed himself with the drinking, in more ways than one.

But he'd given her Birdie, and that was worth it all.

Things happened the way they were meant to happen. She believed that with all her heart.

Only, what did that mean when it came to Penn? What purpose could have brought him back into her life?

The house wants him here.

She didn't believe that one.

There wasn't anything supernatural going on. So what was Penn's game? He'd gone off to New York City and become a high-powered executive. She didn't know the man he was now, just because she'd known the boy. It had to be an old will he had in his possession.

So why was she so scared to take a look at it and show him hers? Maybe it would clear everything up.

Maybe not.

The truth had always been scary.

She liked to fool herself that she'd grown up and changed, but she hadn't, not much, at least not deep down. She'd never told anyone about her stepfather's abuse, or about how she'd really gotten pregnant when she was eighteen, or what a rotten husband Jared had been—and a whole host of smaller things in between that she was too ashamed to admit. Sometimes, she even blamed other people, like Otto, but he had been more like her partner in lies than anything else.

Otto had taken responsibility the only way he could, so many years after the fact. He'd left her this farm. It was what was supposed to make everything right. As if anything could ever do that.

A stab of self-hatred hurt deep inside, and she hugged Birdie close. Her daughter was one of the few things in her life she could take true pride in. She couldn't lose Birdie's home.

Maybe, if she told Penn how much the house meant to her, they could work something out no matter how things turned out with the conflicting wills.

You're pretending you can't stand me, but that's not the way you feel at all, is it?

She took her arm out from around Birdie and flopped onto her back on the bed in the dark room. Penn wasn't going to want to work anything out with her. He wanted revenge.

And he was right about one thing. She was the one who'd made things worse.

It was cold in the old pump house. Waiting through the storm was a test of patience. Penn was here. Not in the plan, but the stupid man hadn't taken the hint. And so, now maybe they could be handled as two birds with one stone. But some rethinking would be required.

There was plenty of time to rethink. There was no getting off Limberlost tonight, for anyone. The situation had its advantages. No one was going to get in, either, and who knew when that would change. The river would be high tomorrow. With any luck, the road would be washed out. Help came slow to the backwater boonies.

Yes, it was time for a new plan. Waiting it out here hadn't been the original plan, but nobody had expected a storm this bad, and all things considered, it was a decent strategy. The pump house was dry, if not warm, abandoned years ago by the gas and oil companies that had once made a booming business here. Coming up the hill the back way on the old oil track meant the four-wheel drive was right here, with the couple of water bottles and small boxes of raisins and crackers in the glove box. It was, in fact, a fitting shelter, all things considered. Fate. The past, the present and the future, all together.

Penn and Willa weren't getting out of here alive.

And the little girl... Well, that was just too bad. They were interlopers, all three of them.

They'd get what they deserved.

Chapter 6

Willa woke up to the sound of rain pattering on the metal roof of the farmhouse.

The light coming through the window of her bedroom looked an ethereal gray: filmy, pale and otherworldly. She lay there for a long beat, trying to convince herself to get up and face the day. *Face Penn.*

She had to stop making things worse and start making things better. She'd dug herself a big hole last night, and she had to climb out of it, as painful as that sounded.

Birdie was still sleeping, her stuffed bear clutched against her cheek. Mop stretched out at the end of the bed, opening her mouth in a big cat yawn that said she didn't want to get up, either. Willa slid carefully off the bed. She'd slept in a T-shirt. She pulled a sweatshirt over it and grabbed jeans, then ran her fingers through her sleep-wild hair in a vain attempt to tame the mess.

Well, vamping Penn was hardly in her plans, so what difference did it make if she looked a wreck? But of course she cared. She wanted Penn to look at her and be sorry.

Surely, that was just normal female instinct, when it came to an old flame. Not that she wanted Penn to notice her or think she was attractive. Not at all.

Maybe a little bit.

How awful was that? And totally unexplainable, in any way that could be defended.

It seemed like eons since she'd actually thought about her appearance, or how a man would see her. Hadn't all the trouble in her life come from men? And looking pretty. That had done her more harm than good, since she was ten years old, which was right around the time her stepfather had started noticing.

She turned away from the mirror and crept to the door, turning the handle and then shutting the door behind her quietly. Down the stairs, she found the kitchen just as she'd left it last night, which was slightly messy—and somehow still exuding Penn's presence. She stuck the pot in the sink under the faucet and realized they'd used up what water had been in the tank, and the well wouldn't run without electricity. Somebody had to go outside and turn on the gasoline-powered generator or they'd have no water today.

And that somebody was her.

She headed for the mud room off the back of the house and grabbed a jacket and boots.

"Hey."

Her stomach jumped into her throat. She spun.

Penn stood in the doorway behind her.

Jumpy. She was so jumpy. It was ridiculous.

"I'm going outside to turn the generator on."

"Why don't you let me do that?"

He stood there all lean and darkly good-looking. His face had developed carved-in, solid lines of adulthood over the past fourteen years, which only made him look better. Age did that on men. In the gray morning light she could see specks of silver in his hair. She'd bet he worked a hundred hours a week in the city. He'd always been a driven person. She worked hard, too. But that city life? It was not for her.

Neither was Penn.

Yet, just looking at him had her body tingling and her brain taking an unexpected vacation.

"I can handle it," she said.

"Why don't you get that chip off your shoulder, Willa, and let somebody give you a hand?"

Maybe she would, if it wasn't *him*. Though probably not. Aside from Otto, the last person she'd allowed to help her had been Jared. Look how that had turned out.

"I said I can handle it," she repeated, jerking on the jacket, stuffing one foot, then another, into heavy boots. She whipped around, put her hand on the door.

His hand came down on top of hers.

She froze.

"You're touching me," she said. She sounded breathy, even to herself.

He didn't stop touching her. In fact, he touched her more. He slid his arm around her, twisting her to face him.

Up close.

Right there.

A breath apart.

She stared straight at him, caught by the strange, searching look in his eyes. Her heart zinged and her nerve ends went from tingling to full-blown fire.

"What do you want?" she asked, still breathy in a harsh, raspy way.

The line of his hard mouth twitched, almost a smile, but not quite. Too serious. It was true, what she'd thought before about not knowing him. She'd let him stay in her house because of circumstances, never thinking of her safety. It was Penn. She knew Penn. But she didn't—not really.

He could have turned into a serial killer, for all she knew. Which somehow sounded slightly more safe than what was apparent—that he'd definitely turned into a heartthrob.

"I want you to let me do something for you," he said finally.

"Why?" *Oooh, bitterness.* She sounded so suspicious. And she was.

She hadn't done anything to deserve any kindness from him. She'd been planning to force herself to play nice today, but she hadn't expected him to play nice first.

And for all she knew, he wasn't. He probably had some ulterior motive.

"Because it needs doing?" he asked. "Because I'm here and you don't have to do everything by yourself?"

"I'm fine. I can take care of myself and Birdie just fine."

"I'm here."

"Doesn't change anything."

"Seems to me it changes everything."

Now what was he talking about?

"Stop talking in riddles," she snapped.

He stood there with his feet firmly planted on the floor, her body trapped between his and the door, his grip still on her arm. She could fight her way out of this spot, but she'd feel like an idiot. And he was stronger, she knew that.

"We don't have to be enemies, Willa. If I can let the past go, so can you. I want to work together, to figure out what's going on with the will—and to wait here until the weather lets up. Maybe," he finished—

and that twitch at the corner of his mouth came again,
"I'm just trying to kiss your ass."

She blew out a disbelieving breath.

"Then let me bend over so you can do it properly,"
she jabbed at him.

The look in his eyes then got her heart beating so
fast, she had a second's terror she'd hyperventilate.
Yeah, he was *so* right, she had a way of making everything worse than it had to be.

"Go ahead," he said.

That did it. She pushed against his chest—hard,
taking him by surprise—and whipped around to
grab the doorknob. She was out the door before he
could stop her.

Or maybe he didn't want to stop her, since it was
crazy to think he couldn't do anything he wanted to
do. Maybe he'd accomplished everything he had in
mind, which was to completely and totally discom-
bobulate her by making her feel some horrible sexual
connection—one that, he had no way of knowing,
she was already feeling.

Sex. She hated sex, even though it was good, had
been good—with Penn at least—which had to be the
only reason she couldn't look at him without *thinking*
sex. But sex was just another way people controlled
each other. She should know….

And Penn was controlling her, just by making her
feel hot when he touched her. And he said things that
got just a little too close to being suggestive.

Or maybe that had been her. Dammit. She stomped through the muddy yard to the shed out back, where she switched on the generator, then stomped back, cursing Penn in her head all the way. Then she cursed herself for good measure.

He was in her kitchen, *her* kitchen, measuring coffee grounds into the coffeemaker when she got back. Apparently, he was determined to be helpful.

"Generator's on," she said briefly. "We should have water now. We can't run too much electricity, though. The generator can't handle everything."

"I remember," he said. "I spent a lot of time here when I was a kid, Willa."

She shrugged. "Okay."

He ran water in the pot and finished fixing the coffee, then punched the on button. Wind creaked outside and the sound of brewing mixed with the noise, which still left a huge, gaping void in the room.

Leaning against the counter now, he crossed his arms.

"What happened to Jared? I'm just curious," he added, as if he expected her to attack him for the question.

It was a fair question. He and Jared had been friends once, though they had broken off contact after the wedding.

And it was an easier question than some of the others he might ask.

"He died."

His expression didn't change, though she detected a flicker in his eyes that she couldn't decipher.

"I'm sorry to hear that," he said. "Was it an accident, or—"

"You could call it an accident."

"What does that mean?"

"He ran his car off the road, down an embankment. Hit a tree."

"That wasn't an accident?"

"He was drunk." Her words sounded bitten off, angry, even to her. But she wasn't sure angry was exactly the right word.

Disgusted might be a better one.

And definitely not sad, for which she felt guilty.

That was probably where the anger came from. A little bit of anger at herself for that not-so-honorable feeling about Jared's death.

"You weren't in the car?" Now *he* sounded almost angry.

She shook her head. "I was home with Birdie. He went out for milk. Apparently he got milk *and* beer. A state trooper called around midnight, after someone saw his car. I'd gone to sleep, so I didn't realize he hadn't come back."

And then he never came back....

"Was that something that happened all the time? Was Jared a drunk?"

Yes, he definitely sounded angry.

She shrugged. She hadn't really wanted to get

into this. "He was probably an alcoholic, though I'm hardly qualified to say. But yeah, it happened a lot."

"Why did you stay with him?"

Was he angry at *her?* His gaze pinned her and didn't let go.

"Relationships are complicated." She knew that wasn't a real answer. "We were married. It didn't really get that bad till later, and then I was pregnant with Birdie. And I was grateful to him. It's complicated." She'd already said more than she should have, so she stopped.

"Grateful?"

"Can we just not talk about this?" Talking to Penn about Jared and her marriage was weird and difficult.

He backed off, surprising her, but he came right back on another tack.

"Was that when you moved in with Otto, after Jared died?"

"No. That was a couple of years ago when Jared died. We were living in an apartment in town. We didn't move in with Otto until last year."

"How did that come about?"

Oh yeah, he had more questions, and they were going to get progressively harder. The coffeemaker grumbled as it brewed. Outside, the wind blew around the farmhouse. She didn't like where the rest of this conversation was liable to go.

"It was his idea."

"I didn't say it wasn't, Willa."

She swallowed hard. *Okay, get a grip. Try not to sound so suspicious and defensive all the time,* she told herself.

Even if she *was* suspicious and defensive. All the time.

And proud. She could feel the instinctive lift to her chin she couldn't quite restrain.

"We didn't have any money," she explained. "Jared hadn't worked in a long time and we had a lot of debt. He'd done some stupid stuff, bought an expensive truck just before he lost his job. Bought a four-wheeler. A fishing boat. I sold all that stuff after the accident, but I couldn't sell it for what was owed on it, so I was making a lot of payments, and I had to pay for Birdie's child care. I was working at the garden center."

She saw him grimace, saw the pity enter his eyes, and she couldn't stand to watch his face anymore. She stared at the old metal rooster decorating the counter beside the coffeepot.

She'd made a mess of her life, that's what he was hearing. No college education, no decent job, no decent husband, rolling in debt. And here was Penn, Mr. Big Shot from New York.

"Why are you embarrassed about that, Willa?"

Damn him. She whipped her hot gaze to his. "I'm not embarrassed," she lied.

"Sure you are."

"I worked. I've always worked."

"Did I say you didn't?"

Deep breath. He was right. She was overreacting. Again.

"I'm trying to make our lives better now," she said. *Defensive again!* She couldn't win for losing. "Or at least simpler. Anyway…Otto came into the garden center one day and we got to talking. He sounded lonely. I hadn't seen him in a while, and he offered to let me bring Birdie out to the farm to see his horse."

And he'd felt guilty for how her life had turned out and he knew he'd played a part in it.

But she wasn't going to explain that to Penn.

"And then he offered to let you and Birdie move in," Penn prompted. He furrowed his brow, but not in suspicion, just curiosity.

Or at least, that's how she read his expression. He seemed to be thinking, but it was contemplative, not accusatory.

"It didn't happen just like that," Willa said. "I'm sure he thought about it for a while, and I thought about it, too. I wanted something better for Birdie, and Otto couldn't take care of this place anymore. He said he'd let us live here, and I'd take care of the house and the farm. I wouldn't have to put Birdie in day care anymore. At least not after I got the debts paid off. I kept working for the first six months after we moved in, and I was able to put all the money into paying down the debt. I took care of things around here. I got his herb garden growing again and planted a big vegetable garden. I sell the produce at local farmers' markets. I can jams and make candles and sell them, too."

Penn glanced at the candles in the room. "You made these?"

He sounded impressed, but that was silly. Nothing she did could compare in his world. But he did look interested, and she couldn't help the rush of excitement she felt. She had plans, lots of them, and hardly ever did she have a chance to talk about them.

"Yeah, I made those. And I want to get some chickens this year, and some miniature goats. Otto got some cattle again, and I've been working on some plans to make the farm self-sustaining. At least, if you live simply, which we do. I've saved up a little money and I want to start a real business, a greenhouse—"

A flush warmed her face. She'd gotten too excited there for a minute.

"I'm sure you're not interested in all that," she said.

The coffee was ready. She got a mug down and poured a cup.

"Maybe I am."

She rolled her eyes. "Right. That's why you want the farm. So you can raise chickens."

She realized her mistake right away. Of all the questions Penn could ask, pointing him back to the one about the will was the last thing she wanted to do.

Flicking him a glance, she was surprised to see a smile drifting across his lips—and stunned to feel the way that look made her stomach drop. He *was* good-looking, no way around it...*and when he smiled?* That only reminded her of the Penn she had known so long ago.

And it set her rebellious nerve ends to tingling again.

Then his look sobered. "I want to sell the farm," he said point-blank.

"I know." *What else could he possibly want with it?*

"I'd give it to you if I could. For you and Birdie."

Was that her jaw hitting the floor?

"You would not."

"How would you know that?"

"Because you hate me."

His sharp gaze darkened.

She felt a pang and had to look away.

Focus on the point, she reminded herself. He'd just admitted that if he had the legal ownership of this farm, she and Birdie were losing their home. All her ideas about playing nice were dead and gone.

"I don't hate you, Willa."

Emotion tugged a little harder. She shook herself.

"Well, there's no point discussing it. Whatever will be, will be." And here she'd been all ready to fight, to beg, if necessary, for her and Birdie to keep their home. But he was set on selling.

"I want to open my own firm," he went on. "I need the startup cash."

She could understand his need for independence. She didn't know much about what he did in the big city, but he was smart and clearly ambitious. Otto had always gone on and on about how successful Penn was in his career.

A gasp came out of her then. "Wait! In the will I have, Otto left you money. A lot of it. Couldn't you start up your own company with that?"

If her will was correct, why would he even want to fight it? They could both get what they wanted.

"I want to see your will," he said.

Maybe all this playing nice was worth something after all. Excitement charged her veins. Maybe he wouldn't even fight the will if hers gave him the cash he needed. Suddenly, showing him the will sounded like an excellent idea.

"Hold on." She ran out of the kitchen, down the hall, to the room Otto had used as a study. Pulling open a drawer, she reached inside for the folded envelope that held the will, then raced back to the kitchen.

"Here it is." She whipped the papers open, practically shoved them at him.

He took them and her heart choked in her throat. This was it. Everything was going to be okay.

"This will is dated the same day as mine," he said.

How could that be? She still didn't understand that, or where two wills had come from to begin with.

"Willa."

He looked up, his inscrutable gaze piercing her. A stab of dread went through her.

This wasn't the expression she was hoping for.

"In the will I have, he left the same to Jess and Marcus—funds to Jess, the other property to Marcus. And the farm to me."

"And in this one, he leaves the farm to me but he leaves you all those other funds."

But Penn was shaking his head. "He doesn't own those stocks anymore, Willa. He sold them out years ago, and even then they weren't worth the paper they were printed on."

"Maybe he bought them back!"

There had to be an answer!

But Penn was still shaking his head. "He stopped trading years ago. He wasn't as sharp as he used to be, and he was sharp enough to know it. He cashed out his stocks, put them in stable funds and bonds. That's what he left to Jess—in both wills."

"That can't be true." Desperate, oh yeah, she was desperate. She'd had the perfect solution in her hands and now… "That can't be true because—"

"It means my grandfather essentially disinherited me," Penn finished for her. "Because, to leave me nonexistent stocks is the same thing."

His eyes were dark and hot now. *He* was angry. At his grandfather or at her, she didn't know.

Then she *did* know.

"Why would he do that, Willa? If this will you have is true, why would he disinherit me? Why would he leave Limberlost to you, anyway? How lonely *was* he?"

Chapter 7

Penn didn't have to wonder whether Willa grasped the implication of his angry, impulsive question. He could see it in her drained, white face and stark, shocked eyes.

"Get out. Get off this farm." She flung the order at him, as if she had the right.

"This is my farm."

"We don't know that yet. And you're not going to stand here and insult me. I wasn't having sex with your eighty-nine-year-old grandfather, if that's what you're suggesting. And don't even pretend you weren't suggesting it!"

She whirled, ready to march off. He grabbed her

arm, held her tightly. She wasn't going anywhere. He wanted answers.

"Then why would he leave you this farm? *If* he left you this farm." He'd been leery last night, suspicious. He'd let that feeling subside, let other feelings take over. Old, crazy feelings. Sympathy. Curiosity. Sentiment. *And dammit, maybe a little desire.*

"We have two choices, it appears. Either my grandfather disinherited me in favor of you, or this will is a fake. Well…I suppose there is a third choice. Somehow, you tricked him into signing it."

"None of the above," she bit out, eyes flashing. "Let go of me."

"Then explain it to me!"

Emotion-charged air hung staticlike between them. Hurt flared in her hot eyes.

"Go to hell!" She yanked her arm, hard, out of his grasp and pushed past him.

"Run, Willa. Go ahead, run."

Her ramrod-straight back stopped. She pivoted, then came back and snatched the will off the counter where he'd left it.

"I am not running," she hissed at him. "I will not run from this fight. Otto left me this farm—for me and for Birdie. You have to be wrong about those stocks, that's all."

"And if I'm not?"

"A court can decide which will is legal."

"I want to know why my grandfather would leave

you this farm, Willa. I want an explanation. Now." He forced himself to keep his tone calm, even as his veins pounded with anger, resentment—and, yeah, pain. He'd never given much thought to his inheritance from his grandfather, but discovering he might have been left with nothing was a slap in the face.

He'd loved Otto, even if he hadn't enjoyed him so much. And he'd believed the old man loved him.

And yeah, he'd just lost his temper, completely, and he was already angry at himself about that.

He tore his gaze from Willa, working to control the stew of feelings inside him. Why would his grandfather leave him to discover this cruel slap after his death?

It didn't make sense.

And Willa wasn't giving him any explanations.

He snapped his gaze back to her, not sure what to say next. Stunned, he saw the tears glistening in her eyes, and he couldn't say anything for a painful moment. She was hurting, too. And he'd caused some of that hurt.

"I don't have an explanation," she said, her voice raw, the anger gone from it. Her hazel eyes were intensely green suddenly, the gold disappearing into tiny, dark flecks. "Maybe there is something you don't know, that neither of us know. You say you know about those stocks, but you could be wrong."

"I'm not wrong."

"Well, something's wrong!" Her voice rose. "He said he'd made sure all of you were well taken care of, that if he left you the farm, you'd just sell it, and he couldn't stand that idea. He didn't want the farm to go to strangers. He wanted someone to have it who would live here, who would love this house, farm this land, remember his stories. He said Birdie and I were as close to family as he had, who would do that after he was gone."

Emotion filled Penn's throat. What she was saying had the ring of truth. Otto had known no one in the family wanted this farm or would keep it. Any of them would sell it. But that didn't explain disinheriting him in her version of the will; and whether she believed him or not, he knew those stocks were long gone.

This whole thing was crazy.

"And I certainly didn't sleep with him to get it," she added fiercely. "I didn't trick him into it, either. But you can believe what you want. I am just a slut, you know."

Her words stung. She looked abused, and suddenly he felt like the abuser.

"I never called you that."

The wind died outside for a moment. It was the past blowing hard around them now.

"I don't want you here," she said flatly.

"Yeah," he said finally. "I know."

Whatever he'd thought would come of seeing Willa again, whatever fantasies had reared their heads, it had turned ugly, fast.

He didn't have to be stuck here, not even by the storm. It was daylight, and it was only a few miles down the road, over the hill, to the hard road that led to the main road through town. There were houses within a few miles. Rain and wind didn't have to stop him. In fact, he was better off on foot. The road was likely washed out by the creeks that would have swelled and crossed it. A car, even if they had one that was serviceable, couldn't make it. But on foot he could go around the washed-out places.

He'd get out of here, get a tow truck back for the Land Rover as soon as the road was passable.

Willa had Birdie to think about, and she'd been living here all this time. He was the one who had to go. At least for now, until they got this thing figured out.

And then? Then, could he really turn Willa and Birdie out of this house, off the farm?

He didn't even want to think about it. He didn't want to think about Willa anymore at all.

He just wanted out of here. His emotions were so out-of-control, he could hardly trust himself around Willa.

She said nothing as he walked around her, out of the kitchen, up the stairs. He found heavy work boots, once Otto's, and grabbed his jacket.

He walked out of the house in Otto's shoes and wondered if the same size feet were the only thing his grandfather had left him.

And he refused to let himself wonder why the hell he couldn't stand to look Willa in the eye if they weren't.

* * *

The road was washed out, as he'd expected. He climbed up along the bank of the first creek, pulling himself up by grasping onto rain-soaked tree trunks. The underbrush was thick beneath his boots. He pushed through, came to the ridge of the bank, and stared down, analyzing the trees, what he'd hold on to, where he might slide in the wet undergrowth and leaves. Clambering around on these banks had seemed a lot easier when he was a kid.

The baby bear appeared out of nowhere. Baby black bear.

He hadn't seen one of those in…. Forever, it seemed. For a breath, he was transfixed.

But he also knew what came with them. Mother bears.

He heard a sound behind him, a grunt, or… Animal or human, he wasn't sure. Bear seemed likely—

He had a split second before he felt something powerful slam against the back of his head—and then that path down the bank he'd been strategizing over, those rocks at the bottom of it, were coming right at him, face front, and hard. He hadn't even made it past the farm.

Willa poured Birdie a bowl of her favorite cereal and told herself she wasn't at all worried about Penn. It was hardly dangerous to walk down the road to town. It might be crazy in this weather, but it wasn't dangerous. He probably wouldn't even have to walk that far before he'd find someone who could give him a ride on in. Just a few miles. He'd be soaked, maybe end up sick....

Why was she worrying about him like a mother hen? He was a big boy. He'd made his bed and he could go get wet in it.

"How come you don't like that man?"

She blinked, focused on Birdie. Her little face peered up at her, without her glasses, from her seat at the old, scarred kitchen table. The chairs were big, and they always made Birdie look tinier than she was.

"I didn't say I didn't like him," she answered nimbly, or so she hoped.

She also hoped Birdie wasn't going to go off on a tangent about how the house didn't *want* him to leave. Again. She'd had enough of that last night.

"I don't think you like him," Birdie said.

"I don't like him or dislike him," Willa told her. "I don't know him."

"He said you used to be boyfriend and girlfriend."

Birdie was a persistent little peep.

"That was a long time ago."

"Was he a good kisser?" Birdie popped a spoonful of cereal in her mouth and gave her a grin, mouth full, milk dribbling out the sides.

Willa blew out a frustrated breath. There was a knot in her chest and a bad, very bad, tingle in her veins, just at the thought of Penn Ramsey.

"There won't be any TV today, Birdie, because we can't use the generator for everything. We have to keep the water running and the refrigerator going, so our food doesn't spoil. Now finish up, then we'll find you something to do while I go check on the cows, okay?"

"You didn't tell me if he was a good kisser!"

"You're four! I'm not talking to you about kisses!"

"Mo-mmy?" She dragged the word out into about ten syllables. "What about when I'm five?"

Willa wasn't going there. Anytime she told Birdie she was too young for something, Birdie started reeling off future ages.

"Eat your cereal, pumpkinhead."

She turned away, cutting off the conversation to the best of her ability.

"Six?" Birdie went on. "Seven?" she called. *"Eight?"*

Willa found Birdie's coloring book in the old camp box in the parlor. She had crayons scattered everywhere, but Willa was too tired to clean them up. They'd just end up on the floor again. She dropped the coloring book onto the couch and grabbed up a handful of picture books from the stack on the floor by the rocking chair. There was a little handheld video game stuffed into the couch cushions, but the battery was dead.

She took it back to the kitchen. "We can charge this for a little while so you can play with it later, okay? I got out your books and your coloring things. I want you to stay *right here,* you promise?" She took up Birdie's bowl and snatched a napkin out of the holder and handed it to her. "Wipe your mouth."

She was worried about leaving Birdie alone again. *Look how that had worked out last time.* But it was raining hard, and still windy, and that was life on a farm. You had to tend the animals, whether it was handy or not, weather be damned.

Penn was probably soaked by now.

Not that she was thinking about him or that she felt at all bad that she'd told him to leave. He'd be fine.

And after what he'd said, what he'd implied....

There had never been anything like that between her and Otto, and for anyone to even to suggest it was ridiculous, not to mention insulting. Especially Penn. And yeah, it had stung a whole lot more, knowing how he'd felt about her when they broke up all those years ago. He hadn't called her a slut then, but he'd thought it. She knew he had.

Or at least, she'd thought it about herself.

Come on, Willa, you know you give it up for anybody. Even your stepdaddy.

How Marcus Ramsey had known about her stepfather, she never knew. Penn's cousin had caught her down by the river after a swim. He'd given her a beer, and then another one, and she didn't know to this day why she drank them. She'd never had beer before. It had seemed like fun. Then he'd started telling her she was making him hot and that she'd better stop flaunting herself around him, or she'd get what she was begging for. She wasn't begging for anything, not then. She'd begged later, when he was on top of her.

Don't go there. She forced her thoughts off that track. It hurt too much. It was because of Penn. Thank God she never saw Marcus—hadn't for years. Otto had given him the farm and the house years ago, though the title had only gone to him in the will, and Marcus had stayed away. What Otto had to do with that, she didn't know. Otto never spoke of that day by the river. He'd come down there to the river ford and caught them. Too late. He'd taken her home. He should have taken her to a hospital or the police station, but Otto pretended not to see the obvious and maybe she had, too—until the obvious had become a baby inside of her.

She couldn't blame Penn for not understanding why Otto had left her the farm, but he didn't have to be so offensive. And their past just made that worse. It was true what she'd told him about Otto wanting the farm to go into hands he felt would care for it, love it. The farm meant something to Otto and to her. It just meant dollar signs to his grandchildren, and so he'd left them what he knew they wanted, money to Jess and Penn, that property to Marcus where he'd been living all this time. They'd been well-served. How much money did one person need?

Penn thought those stocks had been sold already. She couldn't believe it. Otto wouldn't have done that. Penn would find out.

Then maybe her deal would still work. He'd go with her will and leave it at that. It didn't matter to Jess and Marcus—they got the same deal either way. This was between her and Penn. Penn would find out he was wrong about those stocks, and they could discuss the situation again.

From afar.

She got her jacket and boots on, and checked on Birdie again.

"Remember, no disappearing, okay?" she told her. "I couldn't find you last night and I was really scared."

"I didn't go anywhere, Mama. I was in your bed," Birdie insisted.

Willa blew out a frustrated breath. "I didn't see you anywhere, Birdie, and you didn't answer me when I called you."

"That's because I was pretending to be invisible, and the house wanted me to be quiet."

Willa felt a tingle creep down her back again. "Birdie!" She didn't know what to say. Birdie's nonsense about the house was just that, nonsense. So, why was it freaking her out? "You have to understand. I was scared. I thought you were missing. Pretending to be invisible and not answering when I call you isn't a good game."

Did this mean Birdie had been hiding under the bed last night? Playing a little game? It wasn't something Birdie had ever done before, and the timing had been really bad, if it was so. But it didn't seem as if she was going to get a straight answer out of her daughter.

"We have to do what the house wants," Birdie said. "It wants to take care of us."

"No, you have to do what *I* want, Birdie. Do not leave the house while I'm gone. And always answer me when you hear me call. Promise?"

Birdie's little mouth formed a stubborn line, but finally she said, "Okay, Mama."

Willa felt like banging her head against a wall.

She went out to the horse barn, then down the hill to check on the cattle. The fence was still up, thank goodness—and lo and behold, the calf was standing in the road, easy as you please, and she got it back to the barn with a scolding. Flash was at her heels the whole way, till he ran off to the far end of the meadow and along the road, barking madly. She didn't know what his problem was, but she wasn't going after him, not in this weather.

Halfway back up the hill, Flash all but barreled into her, something big in his sharp teeth, dropping it in front of her.

She stopped short. Her hood blew off her head in the force of the wind and she wiped at the rain on her face. The sky overhead grumbled.

It was a boot. Flash had dropped a boot at her feet.

And she knew that boot. It was Otto's old work boot.

Otto's old work boot that Penn had been wearing when he left the house.

Chapter 8

Penn was ashen. He looked half-dead, really. Willa's head reeled just a little. She'd run, letting Flash lead her, down the hill, across the meadow, to the end of the farm where the flooded creek rushed across the road, washing it out.

Flash barked, running circles around Penn as she dropped to her knees beside him. He was down on the pebbly bank, just shy of the flooded creek and the rocks. Her heart slammed up into her throat.

"Are you okay?" she cried. "What happened?"

He didn't answer. Oh, God. He needed emergency care. She was barely qualified to care for her cattle. She couldn't walk out herself, not and leave him here—and Birdie! She couldn't leave them alone, not like this.

"We have to get you back to the house!" she cried. "You have to help me! Come on!" The wind blew her words away.

She grabbed at his muscular shoulders, but he didn't move.

Panic ripped at her insides, and she worked to keep her head on straight. She couldn't fall apart right now.

And neither could he. He couldn't lie here in the wind and rain.

Needing to do something, she knelt down and worked his boot back on. Something inside him seemed to snap to comprehension finally, and his hand grappled for hers, trying to get to his feet. He was wet and muddy and heavy, putting so much of his weight on her, she nearly fell to her knees again. He pushed her away.

"I'm okay," he rasped. "I...hit my head. I think I was out."

He was not okay. He shook on his feet and he was sickly pale.

"What happened?" she asked again.

"I saw a bear."

"A bear?" She had the urge to glance around, but she knew the bear had to be long gone.

"Baby bear. I think...something hit me from behind, on the head. The mother..."

Thank God it had left him alone after knocking

him down. She felt sick to think of how it could have torn him apart while he'd been unconscious. Black bears roamed these woods; she'd heard talk about them, but their scarcity made her forget and feel safe. But she was thinking about it now, and walking out on her own to find some help sounded even less appealing, all of a sudden.

First she had to figure out how bad off he was, then she'd see.

"Where are you hurt? Can you walk back to the house?" She looked up at him, feeling the unsteadiness of his feet as he leaned on her.

He looked vulnerable, pale, a scrape across his forehead bleeding red, the rain not doing anything to wash it away.

"Yes, of course," he insisted. "It's just my head."

"Just your head," she said sarcastically.

"I'm all right," he said again.

He didn't look all right, but he sounded determined. She started pulling him along with her up onto the road, helping him whether he liked it or not. It was a long way back to the house, up the hill in the rain, and he was frighteningly pale.

"Just let me sit down a minute," he said when they reached the end of the meadow, at the bottom of the drive that wound up the hill to the house. "You're rushing me."

He wasn't really asking, because he was already reaching for a huge tree trunk, all but sliding down it to sit on the wet ground. The hickory tree was huge, and underneath its canopy the rain filtered, caught in the umbrella of leaves above. He sat with his back to the tree, sheltered slightly from the wind. She knelt in front of him.

His eyes closed a minute, the granite-like planes of his face were etched with strain. He looked exhausted, and she felt guilt slug her hard.

She'd pushed him out of the house. He'd helped her last night, in every way he could, and if he hated her and tormented her for it, she deserved that to some degree, didn't she?

"I'm sorry," she whispered.

She didn't think he'd heard, but his dark eyes flickered open and he stared straight at her. He was ashen, but even so, he was shockingly handsome. More so, in this moment of weakness, when, for just a blip, she didn't feel so scared of him. She was scared *for* him. She wanted to help him, protect him.

"Why?"

"For making you leave."

"You can't make me do anything, Willa."

She felt slapped, and even as she knew she was overreacting, the distance of those words left her sick. *Yeah. She couldn't make him do anything, because he didn't care what she felt or thought about anything.*

What did you expect, Willa? she scolded herself.

She started to push up from her knees and he surprised her by reaching out. Gripping her hand.

"Don't leave," he said.

His gaze caught hers and she saw something in those dark, hard eyes of his. Vulnerability.

"Don't take offense at everything I say, Willa."

A lump filled her throat.

"Just give me a minute and we'll go on up the hill," he said, his voice low, rough, not pleading but sincere. "Just sit with me for a minute. My head's killing me."

So she sat on the wet ground under the tree, with the rain dripping through the leafy branches above, the wind wrapping around them, hard, then softer, then hard again. They were both a mess, sopping wet, muddy. It didn't matter anymore. There were trilliums blooming on the bank. The wet world around them was so gorgeous, lush and green. She never just *sat* anymore.

"Are you sure you're okay?" she asked Penn. She felt as if she needed to *do* something. "You're bleeding. We need to get that cut cleaned up. You might have a concussion."

"I'm fine. I don't think I was out long. I just hit hard, that's all."

He didn't look fine, but she didn't argue. She hadn't wanted to go to the hospital last night herself.

"I've never seen a black bear," she said.

"I saw one once, when I was a kid," he said. "Scared the crap out of me and I ran, which is not the best thing to do, but I didn't know any better. Otto reamed me good for that."

"I always forget there *are* bears out here."

"There aren't many."

She made a mental check to talk to Birdie about it. She let her run around outside the farmhouse, but she didn't allow her to go very far. Still, the incident terrified her.

"You should talk to Birdie."

"I was just thinking that!" she told him.

He reached up, touched the bloody scrape on his forehead.

"It looks gruesome," she told him. "Just so you know."

"Thanks." He grimaced.

"You have to stay here now. You can't leave. It was a stupid idea to start with."

"It's strange how I can't seem to get off this farm."

Yes. It was strange. Willa didn't like the ripple that thought sent down her spine. She was being silly. Birdie's nonsense was getting to her, maybe. What was she thinking, the house didn't want him to leave? That was ridiculous. "Oh, well, maybe it's the quake," she said cheerfully, not feeling cheerful, but needing to get the nonsense out of her head somehow.

"Quake?"

"Don't you know about the Haven earthquake? It was on all the news. National news. Cable. Everywhere. Last year."

He stared at her a moment. "I guess I vaguely remember Otto saying something about it."

"It was the perfect storm of atmospheric pressure, or some kind of hooey like that. Some paranormal agency came in here and said it had created foundational movement for paranormal activity. There were a lot of strange red lights in the air. People reported all kinds of stuff. The media got very excited. Anything can happen in Haven!"

"I don't remember that part," Penn said.

"That part was pretty ridiculous."

"Yeah. Bad brakes, flat tires, wild storm that never stops, no way to communicate with the outside world. Not being able to find Birdie, when you looked right where she was."

"Are you trying to creep me out?" Willa asked him. Because it was working. Because she couldn't shake the weird feeling she had about it. The house wanted them all to stay right there, so it could *protect* them. And look what had happened to Penn when he'd tried to leave.

Stop it, she told herself.

And yet the creeped-out feeling didn't go away.

"It's just…" Penn's sentence trailed off.

"Just what?"

"You got pretty upset when Birdie said the house wanted us here."

"Because it's nonsense," Willa said quickly. "I know you don't believe that."

"Do you?"

"Of course not!"

"Did you see those red lights?"

She shrugged. "Well. Yeah. But that doesn't mean anything. It was a bad storm, and it was some strange atmospheric conditions, I guess. I don't think that means Limberlost has some kind of magic to it now, or that the house wants us here, or wants anything for that matter. If it did, it would be nice if it told us what it was!"

"Maybe the house has its own way of doing things."

"You're going to make me start thinking you have some serious brain damage," she said. "Or that you're as imaginative as Birdie. She told me a little while ago that the house wanted her to be invisible last night and not answer me when I called her."

Penn stared at her. "They say kids feel paranormal activity more than adults. Their young minds are more open to it."

"I've heard that, too. That doesn't mean I believe it."

"All right," he said suddenly. "Come on. Let's go. I just needed a minute to let my head stop swimming."

She bit her lip. He was lying about being fine, she knew it. And his head must still be swimming, the way he was talking. There was nothing supernatural going on. She shouldn't have brought it up. It was supposed to be a joke, or a way to vent the creepy feeling she'd had after that conversation with Birdie. It hadn't worked.

"The river's flooded," he said. "Just in case you

didn't check. There's no way to cross it right now, and the road back to town's washed out, with the creeks so high."

"I know." She knew what he was telling her. They weren't getting out of here, and no one was getting in. Unless the phones came back, they'd be out of touch until the water went down.

The drive was steep, and she was relieved when the house came into view around the curve. She was worried about Penn, but she was worried about Birdie, too.

Her feet moved quicker as they reached the porch, and she almost collapsed in gratitude when she opened the door and saw Birdie neatly curled up with her coloring book, her lower lip tucked under her teeth as if in deep thought. The little girl perked up when she saw Penn come in with her.

"He's back! You *do* like him!"

Sometimes, having a four-year-old was an exercise in total humiliation.

Penn lifted a brow. A bleeding brow.

"Come on." Willa grabbed his arm again. "I want to look at that scrape."

"Why is he hurt? What happened?" Birdie jumped up and was right on their heels, as close as Flash.

She had twenty more questions, and she nearly died of excitement when she found out a *bear* was involved.

Despite Flash and Birdie being underfoot, Willa managed to get Penn onto the stool in the kitchen, where she washed the cut—relieved when she found it wasn't quite as terrible as it looked. It had just been the blood.

"You might actually need stitches," she told him. "You're going to have a scar."

"That'll just make me more interesting," he said. "Rugged and rough. A little bit dangerous."

"Oh, sure." She tried not to laugh. And damn him, he was probably right. He was definitely dangerous, at any rate.

He let Birdie put a cartoon princess bandage on the cut, then she gave him a little kiss on top of it, up on her tiptoes. It was very sweet, and very cute, and Willa told herself it was just that Birdie had never met a stranger. She was outgoing.

But the truth was, her daughter had adored Penn from the start. And he was good with her. Patient.

She wasn't so much annoyed anymore as she was... Sad.

Sad because Birdie didn't have a father. Sad because maybe, if things had been different, Penn should have been...

And she had to cut her thoughts off right there, with that.

"I think you should rest now," she told Penn.

"Putting me to bed?"

He said that and just looked at her as if he wasn't implying anything more. And he wasn't, was he? She just thought *sex* every time she looked at him.

She didn't even *like* sex, for pity's sake! Not anymore. Not since that day by the river with Marcus.

"You were knocked out. In the rain. By a bear. I think you should go lie down."

"I'll read you a story!" Birdie offered.

She couldn't read, but that wasn't the point. She knew a lot of her story books by heart.

"I'd love that," Penn said.

Dammit, that was sweet of him. In spite of everything she'd put him through and had happened to him, he was sitting here being kind to a four-year-old.

"Go pick out some stories," Penn said.

Birdie raced off to the parlor for books.

"Thank you," Willa said.

"Hey, she's the one helping me out. Keeping me entertained. Saving me from nap time."

"You can still lie down, and you should."

Penn pushed up off the stool. He might lie and tell her he was fine, but she noticed he moved a little slowly, a little stiffly.

He took her by surprise when he reached out and tucked a finger under her chin, looked at her steady in the eyes. Her breath caught and she couldn't have moved if she'd tried.

"I come all the way from the big city and have to tell you to relax, Willa?" he said quietly.

She didn't know what to say, since lying about how relaxed she was wasn't going to fly. Obviously, he could tell she was tense and nervous and on edge.

Admitting *he* was the cause wouldn't help matters, either.

"You're about to get offended now, aren't you?" he said. He let his hand drop.

He wasn't touching her anymore, and dammit, she'd liked it. Just that teeny, little tender touch. She'd *liked* it.

She swallowed hard. "No."

"All right," he said, his voice still soft. "Then I'm making progress, aren't I?"

"Progress to what?" she blurted out. Not a question she really should be asking, but there it was. She wanted to know the answer.

"I don't know."

Penn left her with that, not sure of the wisdom of putting into words what he was thinking. He'd been as angry with her as she'd been with him when he'd left to hike off the farm, but he knew that was heat-of-the-moment anger. He didn't know what was going on, but whatever it was, he didn't think Willa had perpetrated a fraud. There was too much honest pain in her eyes, under all those secrets that he saw there, too.

If he was going to figure out what was going on here, he'd have to get to those secrets. There was time, since he was definitely not going anywhere else, at least not today.

But breaking through Willa's barriers... That wouldn't be easy.

He didn't want to think he was using the little girl. She was cute, and she looked so much like Willa she took his breath away at odd moments. Birdie was an innocent, a younger Willa—one without all those barriers.

She propped herself on her elbows on the bed beside him and turned the pages of her story book, reciting obviously memorized lines off the pages, missing some, clearly making up others. She was an inventive, engaging child.

And she was Jared North's. He tried not to think of that, or how shabbily Jared had ended up treating Willa. He couldn't be happy Jared was dead, but he was glad he was out of Willa's life.

"How did you get the name Birdie?" he asked when she read "the end." She'd already picked up another book.

He wanted to hear a story, but not one out of her stack of books.

She put the book down, and with her little fists propped under her chin, said, "I was born early. My real name is Earlene, after my grandma who's dead. Both of my grandmas are dead. And I don't have any grandpas, either, except Mr. Otto, and he's dead, too. And my daddy is dead."

It was a long list of people she'd lost from her life, but other than a little crack in her voice when she'd mentioned Otto, which she recovered from quickly, she seemed okay. He had to think Willa was a pretty good mother, to make up for so many missing people in Birdie's life. He hadn't thought about Willa's parents, her mother and stepfather, so it was a shock to hear they'd passed away. Her biological father had left her mother when Willa was a baby, so he supposed that when Birdie talked about her grandpas on Willa's side, she meant Willa's stepfather.

In spite of the small town where everybody knew everybody's business, Willa's family had kept to themselves. They'd been poor but hardworking, by all accounts. Her stepfather worked in the oil fields and wasn't home much, and her mother had taken in sewing at their small house up the road. If Willa knew how to work hard and live frugally, she'd come by it honestly.

"Mama said cuz I was born three weeks early and my name was Earlene, she called me her early birdie," the little girl went on. "And she said I ate like a little bird, so then she just started calling me Birdie. Now everybody calls me Birdie."

"Do you like it?"

"Uh-huh." Birdie nodded emphatically. "I'm the only Birdie I know."

She was an original, that was for sure—not that he spent any time around small children. But he liked this one, which was somewhat of a surprise. Not that he despised children. Mostly, he'd just never thought about them.

"No brothers and sisters? You like it that way?" Now he was poking.

"Nope. Well, Mama had another baby a long time ago. But it died before it was born."

So. That's what had happened to the child Willa had been carrying fourteen years ago. And despite his curiosity being satisfied, Penn felt a nudge of disgust with himself for manipulating the information out of a four-year-old.

"You like living on the farm?" he asked, changing the subject.

"Uh-huh!" Birdie nodded emphatically again. "We get to keep it. Mr. Otto said so!"

He hadn't expected that; but if he'd been thinking more clearly past the ache still pounding in his head, he should have known that if Otto had promised Willa the farm, Birdie might have heard it from him, too.

A sound from the door alerted him before Willa stepped inside the room. Too late though, for her not to assume he'd been prying information out of her child.

Hell, he *had* been prying information out of her child. Just not that last bit, that's all.

"Birdie," Willa said firmly. "You need to leave Mr. Ramsey alone now and let him get some rest. He hurt himself, remember?" she added, prompting Birdie to get up.

Before she left, Birdie leaned over, smelling all little-girl soapy and fresh, and kissed him on the top of the head again.

"That'll make it all better!" she said, and bounced off the bed.

Willa shooed her out of the room, and the dagger look in her eyes told Penn everything was definitely not all better.

"Don't be asking Birdie questions," Willa snapped when the little girl was gone. "Leave her out of this. She thinks we're living here forever—"

"I didn't tell her any different."

"I don't care what you told her. I don't want you telling her anything, or asking her questions."

"What are you afraid I'm going to find out, Willa?"

Seriously, she was way too prickly, edgy and nervous. What the hell was going on? It was more than the will, had to be. *Oh yeah, he had questions*...and the more answers he got, the more questions he had.

"Just mind your own business, that's all."

"What are you scared of, Willa?"

He knew suddenly that he wasn't going to stop asking that question till he got an answer.

"I'm not scared of anything."

"Oh, you're scared of a lot of things, Willa, and not just about that will."

"I'm afraid you had some brain damage in that fall," she said sharply. "Like *that* answer?"

"I like your sense of humor, Willa."

Her only response was the door slamming as she left the room. A light, restrained slam, not the loud one she wanted, he was certain.

Outside, the rain still poured down. Spring always

meant a lot of rain in West Virginia, but this was something else.

He and Willa and Birdie were stuck together in this house for a while longer, and right now that was okay with him. He wanted more time to find out the truth Willa was hiding. The will could wait. He was almost more interested in Willa now. An uncomfortable realization, but true. Surely, he really had had some brain damage in that fall. He was supposed to be obsessed with his career. And he was supposed to be angry with Willa.

Why did both of those things seem so empty suddenly?

Chapter 9

Willa made soup. A great big pot of potato soup. She fed Birdie lunch, then tucked her in for an afternoon nap, and resisted the urge to check on Penn. Hopefully, he was sleeping and would sleep until the next day when, again hopefully, it would stop raining. They could use the phone and find a way to get him out of here.

What if he did sleep until the next day? Hadn't he been sleeping for hours now? What if he did have a concussion? Wasn't she supposed to wake him up every once in a while, check on his pupils or something?

And then she couldn't stop worrying, so....

She went back up the stairs, tapped very lightly on his bedroom door, and called his name. She didn't hear a thing.

Nudging the door open just a bit, she peeked inside. The bed was empty.

He'd disappeared, was her first thought, then she told herself to stop being a dummy. Birdie hadn't disappeared last night, and Penn hadn't just up and disappeared, either. Man, she was getting spooked over all kinds of ridiculous things. The house hadn't made Birdie disappear, and it wasn't going to make Penn disappear, either.

"Penn?"

No answer. She went out to the hall. Maybe he'd come out of his room while she'd been busy getting Birdie down for her nap.

She heard a door shut down below.

The front door.

She raced down the stairs and pulled open the door. She saw Penn, bundled up in one of Otto's rain jackets, headed toward her truck.

Willa sped to the end of the porch, not eager to go out in the rain, and yelled against the wind.

"What are you doing?" *You idiot,* she wanted to add.

She figured he didn't hear her. Or want to hear her. She wrapped her arms around herself, the biting wind and chilly rain bringing spring temperatures down to a reminder of winter.

He was looking at her tire, the flat one. Then he

went around and looked at the spare. He came running back to the porch and bounded up the steps.

She moved back, realizing he'd run with his head down against the wind and rain, and was about to barrel into her.

"Hello!" she shouted at him. "It's pouring! And it's not like you can fix my tires. So what the hell are you doing?"

Under the porch, he fixed his steady, searing gaze on her. The cartoon bandage on his forehead looked ridiculous. And sexy.

That she thought the cartoon Band-Aid looked sexy was even more ridiculous.

Why couldn't she just stay mad at him all the time?

"I know I can't fix it," he said.

"Then what were you doing?"

"Just looking," he said. "Just…looking."

She frowned at him, not satisfied, but he brushed past her toward the door. She had no choice but to follow him in if she wanted to know more.

"I was worried about you," she admitted, shutting the door behind her as she came in. He was already shrugging out of Otto's jacket. "I went to check on you. I was afraid if you slept too long you'd lose consciousness or something. If you had a concussion."

She had no idea what she was talking about. A nurse, she was not.

"That's sweet, Willa. I don't have a concussion. I have a headache."

"You had to have hit pretty hard. You were out! And you could hardly walk up the driveway, coming back."

"I'm fine now. But thanks for worrying," he added.

Well, she was half-sorry she'd admitted that, especially since he was looking at her that way. That way that made her tingle with a feeling she'd almost forgotten. She'd also almost forgotten that the last time they'd spoken, she'd been irritated with him for prying information out of Birdie, which she was so sure he'd been doing.

All sweet and cute with her kid...*right. He was a manipulator, that's what he was.* And she'd better not let herself, or her body, forget it.

Though, what evil purpose he could have to be manipulating her or Birdie, she didn't know—which was a flaw in her plan to stay irritated with him. He wanted to prove her version of the will was invalid, but that was out in the open, wasn't it?

As far as she knew, he didn't have any other purpose here, despite the look in his eyes that made her think he *did* have another purpose, and that it had something to do with her.

But no way was she letting herself think that. He'd gone out of her life fourteen years ago, with a bang, and she'd be a fool if she believed he'd had a fire burning for her all this time, ready to ignite just because he was back in town.

"You're thinking too much, Willa," he said suddenly, softly. "You're always thinking too much."

He was watching her, had been watching her for the entire sixty seconds she'd stood there arguing with herself.

"You look at me too much," she said. "Stop looking at me." Now she sounded like a four-year-old herself.

He laughed. *Damn him.*

"Is that why you're out here by yourself, Willa? You don't like people looking at you?"

"I'm not by myself. I have Birdie."

"You don't have a man."

"I don't need a man. What a sexist thing to say."

She was hugging her arms around herself again. She wanted to step back when he moved toward her, but she bumped up against the closed front door when she tried.

"I bet you could figure out something to be mad at me about, just by looking at me," he said.

"Maybe you have a really irritating personality and you just don't know it."

He stared at her for another interminable instant before he spoke. "Thanks for letting me know. That's very generous of you."

Why couldn't she make him mad? Well, she could, she remembered. He'd been pretty angry when he'd implied there was something going on between her and Otto, or when he'd suggested she might have conned his grandfather into a will that virtually disinherited him. But his ill humors seemed to evaporate pretty quickly. Whereas her own...

Man, she was a pissy female. A bitch. Angry at herself and taking it out on everyone else in the world—that was her.

"I'm sorry," she said. "Sort of."

He laughed at that. "Well, I guess I'll take what I can get."

"Why do you want anything?" Now what had she gone and done? She would have liked to bite that question back, but it was too late.

He came up a step closer and had the balls to put his big, warm fingers under her chin. She tried to jerk away, but he held her still with nothing but his touch. Her nerves went all aflutter.

"I like puzzles," he said quietly.

"You think I'm a puzzle?"

Something flared in his deep, dark eyes. Something tingled again, way down low in her tummy.

"I think you're something, Willa. I just don't know what yet."

Her knees went to jelly on her. Probably the last time a sexy man had looked into her eyes like she was the only thing on the planet had been...

Fourteen years ago. And it had been Penn. She was so *not* experienced with men.

"I'm just an ordinary person," she said, breathy. She hated that. What was wrong with her? Her heart was pitter-pattering stupidly.

What if he kissed her?

What if she *wanted* him to?

"Flesh and bones," she went on. "Blood. Human." Wow, she was babbling. If the words "pee" and "poop" came out of her mouth next, she wouldn't be surprised.

He just went on watching her like she was the only thing in the world, and she was so uncomfortable, she thought her skin might blow off her body.

"Do you remember the time we went mudding in my old pickup truck?" His voice was so low, she wasn't sure if she was hearing his words or just inhaling them. "And my truck got stuck in the creek and we had to walk back to your house. We stopped at the cave with that big waterfall…"

And they took their clothes off and made love right there, under the waterfall, on that hard rock that would kill her if she tried to do that now. Rocks and bugs and dirt didn't stop her back then. It was just part of the adventure.

"I don't remember anything about that," she lied quickly.

"You remember everything about that. I don't think I have ever wanted a woman as much as I wanted you that day."

Her body melted completely. She had to wonder if he was holding her up, just by his fingertips beneath her chin. Otherwise, she couldn't figure out why she was still upright.

"Don't do this to me," she said—begged. She sounded like she was pleading, and humiliating as it was, she couldn't stop herself from going on.

"Don't play these head games with me. I can't handle it."

She knew hot, wayward dampness behind her eyes. If he kept up like this, she was going to start crying, she just knew it.

He broke her so easily. It was frightening.

"I'm not playing," he said softly. "I remember. Every time I look at you, I remember. And I know you remember, too."

"You remember how it ended?" She had to do something to save herself, even if it was to bring up the ugliest thing between them. "What do you think, you can just pick back up where we left off? I guess you think that because I'm such a slut, and you know it. Maybe I still sleep around with every man I see. You're just checking, right? Birdie's napping. You want to take a turn in my bed?" She couldn't stop.

"Do you think if you call yourself a slut first, it'll stop anyone else from doing it, Willa? Or do you really feel that way about yourself?"

"What are you, a therapist?" Now she found the strength to pull her hand up and open-palm shove him away.

She shook all over and felt sick. She strode past him, heading for the kitchen blindly, only she didn't know what she would do when she got there.

Big mistake, because he just followed her, and there was nowhere to go from there, unless she wanted to go outside in the rain. And she just might do that.

She knew he was there, by the footsteps she could just hear over the ragged breaths she was dragging in to stop herself from crying. She sure as hell wasn't turning around to see him.

"I don't think you're a slut, just for the record," he said in the still of the room.

Rain wrapped the house in a continuous, muted patter that was nothing compared to the pounding of her heart.

"I've never called you a slut," he went on. "And so that you know, I've never thought it, either. You think a mistake when you were eighteen years old makes you a slut? You think I'm that much of a jackass?"

She didn't want him to be understanding. That was so much worse. She wanted him to rail at her, tell her she was, indeed, a slut. Then she'd be validated.

Even *she* was impressed with how twisted her logic could be.

"It doesn't matter," she managed finally, still not looking at him. She stared straight ahead, over the kitchen sink, out the window. Still staring blindly because there were tears in her eyes she was fighting to keep from falling.

"I think it does." His voice was closer. "I didn't think I ever wanted to see you again. I thought if I did see you, I would be angry. And I *was* angry, but it's pretty stupid, and I realize that, too."

Was he telling her he forgave her? She wanted that to make *her* angry. She hadn't asked for his forgiveness.

"What do you want?" she whispered thickly. Surely he wouldn't hear her. It didn't matter.

"I don't know," he answered.

And she turned, because she had to, because he was being so achingly honest…and kind. And she wanted that kindness, as much as she didn't want it.

Maybe she wanted that forgiveness, too. As much as she didn't want it. As much as it hurt.

He was the biggest screwup of her life, and he was standing here in her kitchen. And maybe he was offering her a second chance. She didn't know—and he didn't, either. But it was there. Like a thin little feather of hope floating by on the wind that she might catch. If she tried. If she was brave enough.

If she was crazy.

There was pain in that shadowy dark gaze of his that reached toward her across the kitchen.

A crack sounded outside, over the wind and rain and the heavy pounding of her heart. She looked back out the window and saw fire. In the middle of rain, there was fire.

Chapter 10

Willa was out the door so fast he didn't have a prayer of catching her. Once he saw the fire, he understood. She didn't care about the rain, not now. She had a horse in that barn that was on fire. All he could do was help her—and hopefully keep her from killing herself in the process of getting the horse out safely.

He caught up with her at the barn door. She was shaking and soaked, as he was, and he reached past her and lifted the heavy latch. The straw on the floor of the barn was alight, flames licking everywhere. Lightning? He hadn't noticed any lightning today. Even as the rain was dousing the fire on the exterior of the structure, the barn was burning up inside.

She darted straight down the center of the barn, swerving around spots of fire, and he chased after her. Already, he could hear the wild, terrified snorting of the horse. The stall door creaked as the horse railed against it. He grabbed Willa.

"Just let it out," he yelled over the storm and crackling fire. "Just let it out and get out of the way!"

They could catch it later when it calmed down. But for now, he didn't want to see Willa killed, and she looked just crazy-worried enough to try to take hold of the fire-spooked animal. She was a country girl, but her family hadn't kept animals.

"I know what I'm doing!" she yelled at him.

And maybe she did. She had the stall door open and she was out of the way as the mare barreled out, running right through flaming straw, straight out the barn door.

Willa's face in the dancing firelight streaked with tears.

"She'll be back," he said, "and we'll get her sheltered somewhere else. She'll be all right."

Willa nodded, didn't say anything, and he didn't know if she was in shock or just speechless; but they had to get out of there before this whole place came down on them.

"Come on." He took her hand, pulled, and she came with him. There was another cracking sound as they left the barn, a cracking sound that went straight past his ear, and Willa's hand slipped out of his. He wheeled back, and nearly had a heart attack when he saw her fall to the ground.

Had she been shot? Was that a gunshot?

It had sounded like a gunshot.

Even as he reached for Willa, she was back on her feet. She'd merely stumbled. He didn't have time to assimilate what he was feeling, the relief was so huge. And then they ran, out of the rain, away from the fire.

Inside, she didn't stop, just kept going straight through the house to the big, covered front porch where she stood there, dripping, gazing out into the wind-whipped gloam.

"She'll be all right," he said. "She'll come back. She was too scared for us to handle. The rain will put the fire out. It's not going to spread."

She knew that. He knew she knew that. But he didn't want her out there, out where she was easy pickings.

If that had been a gunshot...

If those tires had been cut by a human hand, not something sharp on the drive...

He hadn't been able to tell for sure, in the poor light and rain.

If that hadn't been a bear that had knocked him cold by the creek...

Maybe he was thinking crazy. Maybe he wasn't. Had lightning set that barn on fire, or...?

He didn't know what to think. Nothing much had made sense since he'd arrived at Limberlost.

"We need to get inside, Willa. Get dry, before we get sick."

She looked at him, something hollow and scared in her eyes. "Why does everything keep going wrong?"

"I don't know," he said, and was relieved when she turned and headed back inside. He didn't want to tell her the crazy things he was thinking. And it *was* crazy. What kind of nut would be hiding out here on the farm in this kind of weather, trying to kill them?

"Coming back to West Virginia would be a big mistake."

The text message he'd received was more ominous now. Was somebody after him? Why? Or was somebody after Willa? He was the one who'd been knocked cold at the creek, and that gunshot—if it had been one—had gone past *his* ear. What about his brakes? Was that a mechanical failure or had they been tampered with? He'd rented the car at the airport, so that couldn't be possible—could it? It was Willa's truck that had had the tires slashed. Had someone set the barn on fire to get him outside—or *both* of them outside?

Was someone out to get both of them? He and Willa had had no contact or connection at all until…

The will.

Both of his cousins had been well-served in the will, either way, so that didn't make sense. Besides, then he'd have to believe one of his cousins was a lunatic.

Did someone else have something at stake, someone he wasn't even thinking about?

Or was he just paranoid and dreaming the whole thing up? The more he tried to make sense of it, the more that seemed like the likeliest scenario. It wasn't as if any crazy person out to get them could have created this storm, trapping them here and isolating them, anyway.

Birdie thought the house wanted everyone to stay right here, so maybe the whole thing was a result of supernatural activity and that earthquake. And that made as much sense as anything else.

He followed Willa inside and shut the door, muting the storm outside.

"I guess I'm going to get changed into some dry clothes," she said. "I made some soup earlier, if you're hungry."

"Thanks." He watched her walk up the stairs. She looked exhausted and upset, and he wished he could go after her and make it all better somehow.

But he didn't know how.

Whatever was going on, he didn't like it. He locked the doors—paranoid? Yes he was—then followed her up and changed clothes, too.

When he came down to the kitchen he found her there, heating a pot of soup on the stovetop. No bad guys were pounding at the door. No gunshots coming through the window.

He'd overreacted, he was sure.

But he didn't intend to let his guard down.

It was a domestic little scene, and he had a moment of surreal fantasy in which this was his life—on a farm, with beautiful Willa in the kitchen and their napping daughter upstairs. Was that how it was supposed to be? Would they have lasted, if not for Willa's mistake that had torn it all apart?

What was he thinking? He'd been dying to get out of Haven from the moment he was born, it seemed like. Why was he suddenly turning it into a Norman Rockwell fantasy? He'd always had big-city dreams, and he'd pursued them with every ounce of his being, from earning the right degrees through the long hours at an enormous Manhattan firm. He was poised to open his own firm, and then he'd really hit the big time, make his dreams come true. The pinnacle was within his reach.

He couldn't let a month—or, hell, even a few days—at Limberlost make him lose sight of it.

"What communication have you had with the executor of Otto's estate?" he asked Willa. Their discussion about the will had ended in such rancor, it hadn't occurred to him before to ask her.

"He sent me a letter. I suppose you got a letter, too?" She leaned against the counter, crossed her arms, watched him. Wary.

"What did it say?"

"Just that he would be in touch with me, that he had a full schedule, and that you were out of the country. That there would be a reading of the will later, when you were available, but that he understood Otto had provided all of his heirs with copies of the will. And so on. I can probably find it later, if you want to see it."

"It sounds like the same one I have."

"If I wasn't in the will, then why would he have notified me?" she asked pointedly.

"Maybe because you were living in Otto's house and the house is part of Otto's estate."

"Maybe."

It seemed that line of thought wouldn't get him anywhere. The executor's letter had certainly made no specific references to the will's contents.

"Have you spoken with Marcus or Jess?" he prompted.

"I spoke with Jess, briefly, right after Otto died. She was at his funeral."

"What about Marcus?"

She shook her head. "Somebody said he was sick. I don't know. He wasn't there."

"Did Jess say anything about the house?"

She gave him an odd look. "Are you telling me *you* haven't spoken with Marcus or Jess?"

Was this the part where he was supposed to again be ashamed of the marginal contact he had with his family back in Haven? He resisted the twist of anger.

"I was out of the country. When I got back, I was prepared to come out here as soon as possible. I expected to see Jess and Marcus while I was here."

Maybe he sounded defensive. She picked up on something.

"I was just surprised. I didn't mean anything by it. I thought you guys were close, that's all." She took out a bowl from a cabinet and ladled a helping of soup into it.

"I guess we were, when we were kids," he said. "After my dad passed away and my mom remarried, the family gossip chain stopped flowing. She's in Arizona now, with her new husband, and I don't think she has much contact with any of the Ramseys." And he was too busy working.

"So, we don't know what their copies of the will say." Willa set the bowl of soup down in front of him. She brought him a spoon and some crackers before he could get up.

"I didn't mean for you to wait on me."

"I guess I'm just used to it."

"Waiting on people?"

"Well." She stood there, her hair still damp, strands clinging lightly to her cheeks. She'd put on a big sweatshirt and another pair of jeans, and she looked crazily sexy with no makeup. "Otto had a hard time getting around sometimes, and Birdie's four. I'm used to feeding people."

"I thought he was pretty well, up until he died."

Otto had died in his sleep. Old age. A quick and simple death in his sleep. The best kind, Penn supposed.

He was glad his grandfather hadn't been alone. Glad Willa had been there. And it socked him hard that he should have told her that.

"He was. But he had his frail days. Or maybe he just liked me waiting on him."

Now she smiled, and the light it brought to her eyes about blew him away.

"Anyway," she went on, her expression turning serious again, "I invited Jess to come out to the house anytime and sort through Otto's things, but she said she'd wait till the will was probated, and that she was in no hurry. We didn't discuss the house, otherwise. I guess I assumed she knew, and it was a pretty short conversation. She didn't seem that interested in the house. She didn't visit very often."

"What about Marcus?"

"I didn't talk to him."

"I mean, did he visit often?"

"Never."

She walked away from the table, put a lid back on the soup pot, then straightened some items on the counter.

"Why's that?"

"I don't know. Jess didn't come around much, either. I heard Marcus has been sick a lot. Not from Jess, but just…around. You know. Small town."

He'd had no idea. Marcus had to be pretty sick to

not have come to the funeral. Did his cousin have some kind of serious illness, and he hadn't even heard of it?

"Last I heard, he was still living out on that property Otto left him in the will," Penn said.

"I guess." She turned. "Can we not talk about Marcus? I really don't know anything about him."

Her voice came out sharp, and he held his spoon still over the bowl he'd been about to dip into.

"Do you have a problem with Marcus?"

"No. Of course not. I haven't seen him in years."

She sounded like she had a problem with Marcus. Truthfully, he'd always had a problem with Marcus, too. He was a bum. No ambition. Kind of a jerk when he was a kid. Jess was older, always the sharp one. She'd stayed around Haven, too, and ran some kind of bookkeeping service in town. He was pretty sure she'd helped Marcus, financially, as much as Otto had over the years. Not that he cared. The property Otto had left Marcus was equal in value to Limberlost and equal to the funds he'd left to Jess. They'd been treated fairly. Unless Willa's version of the will was the real one.

He just hadn't had a lot of respect for Marcus, but couldn't have said exactly why. He had no idea what Marcus did out on that property. He just imagined he bummed his entire living off Otto. He had no proof of it.

"I figured he might have come around looking for

money," Penn said. He was fishing now, but was it possible Marcus could be causing trouble, that Marcus could be the one here on the farm? Maybe he had Willa's version of the will and he wanted to get rid of Willa.

The notion was hard to swallow. Marcus had no reason to believe getting rid of Willa would give him Limberlost. There was Penn. And even if he got rid of Penn, too, there was his own sister, who was too sharp to let Marcus take charge of Limberlost if they inherited it together. The whole reason Otto hadn't let Marcus have title to that other property before he died was likely to make sure Marcus didn't sell it and blow the cash.

He could do that now, so going after Limberlost, too, seemed far too ambitious for good-for-nothing Marcus. Plus, he'd have to be quite the cold-blooded killer to be prepared to do away with Penn, Willa and even his own sister. It would have to be a triple blow to get Limberlost.

The whole thing sounded crazier and crazier.

"Otto mailed him some checks now and then," Willa was saying. "That's all I know, really. I don't know anything about Marcus."

And she sure didn't want to talk about him, either.

He took a sip of the soup. It was potato soup, thick and rich with bits of bacon. Peppered bacon, he thought. He'd missed good country cooking.

Willa was a good cook. He didn't know why that

surprised him. He'd never thought about it. There were a lot of things to learn about grown-up Willa.

That he wanted to learn them was the most surprising thing of all. He'd all but asked her to give them a second chance. If someone had told him last week that he would be feeling this way, he wouldn't have believed it.

But that was before he'd seen Willa again.

Was she willing? And was that what he really wanted? Willa was clearly established in her life in Haven. And he was going back to New York City.

"You're a good cook," he said. She was still at the sink, doing something, keeping busy. At least she wasn't tearing out of the kitchen, as if she couldn't bear to remain in his presence. In fact, she seemed to be almost…lingering, as if she wanted to be around him. Which made a nice change. "Thank you for being here with my grandfather. I'm glad you were with him at the end. I'm glad he wasn't alone."

She turned slowly, her gaze unreadable in the low light coming in the window and the dim glow of the candle she'd left burning on the table. She was conserving electricity because they were using the generator.

It felt like a long moment before she spoke.

"Thank you."

"I can't believe it. You took a compliment."

"Don't ruin it." But she was laughing, not angry. And wow, she looked beautiful when she laughed.

He was falling for her. He knew the feeling. He'd had it before, when he'd fallen for Willa so long ago. And he'd never fallen since, not really, not for any other woman.

It was crazy. His life was in New York. What was he thinking?

He was sure that his career wasn't the only reason he shouldn't let himself fall for Willa. It was just the only one he could come up with at the moment.

"I don't know what you're thinking when you look at me that way," she said.

She sounded scared. Maybe she was thinking some of the same things he was.

Maybe one of them needed to say it out loud.

Because, when they got past the anger, there was something real between them, something that had survived all these years.

"I'm thinking," he said quietly, "that I could fall for you all over again."

Chapter 11

"Don't be stupid." Willa's heart was pounding so hard, she expected it to burst right out of her chest at any second.

"I'm thinking that I could fall for you all over again."

What was he, nuts?

"I'm just being honest. Which, granted, can be stupid."

He was looking at her, talking to her, all calm, cool and collected. Like they weren't discussing something totally momentous. And insane.

"Umm, reality check. You just met me again yesterday. Before that, you hadn't had any contact with me in fourteen years. You don't know me."

"I grew up with you," he pointed out.

"So?"

"So I know you. But yes, you're right, it's crazy. Let's forget it."

Disappointment slammed into her. She swallowed hard. Wow, it hadn't been hard talking him out of that, had it?

He went back to eating his soup. After a few minutes in which she picked her jaw back up off the floor, she marched up to the table and took the not-quite-finished bowl right from under his nose and marched back to stick it in the sink.

"I wasn't done," he protested.

"Yes, you are," she said without turning away from the sink to look at him. "You're all done. Stick-a-fork-in-you done. Done for. Good and done."

Then she was all out of ways for him to be done, dammit.

"You're disappointed, aren't you?"

His voice was right there, behind her. Then his arm was right there, around her waist, pulling her to face him. And he was right there, way too close, in front of her.

"You didn't really want to talk me out of that, did you?" he asked.

"Are you playing games with me?"

He regarded her for a long stretch of time, in which she couldn't have taken her eyes off his if wild horses had been dragging her in the opposite direction.

"No. I'm serious. And maybe a little crazy. I feel crazy when I look at you, Willa. You make me wonder what I've been working for all my life and why I left Haven to find it."

"You left Haven because you didn't want to be stuck in this one-horse town all your life. You never wanted to stay here."

"Maybe I thought when I left, I'd be taking you with me."

"We never talked about that."

"We were busy doing other things," he pointed out.

She tingled down deep some more. It was irritating how he did that to her so easily. Yeah, they'd been busy back then. Laughing and playing and making love.

"We're not teenagers anymore," she pointed out right back to him. "And you have lost your mind if you think you'd want to live in Haven again."

"I didn't say I wanted to live in Haven again."

"I don't want to live in New York City. And this is a ridiculous conversation, since we haven't seen each other in fourteen years. We can't just leap into each other's arms like nothing ever happened, like all those years haven't passed, and like we don't have totally different lives now."

"You're trying to talk me out of this again," he said.

"Talk you out of this *what? This* is nothing!"

"Oh, *this* is something."

He was confusing the hell out of her and making

her hot all over at the same time. She was scared to death she was on the brink of a huge mistake that would ruin her peace of mind forever.

She'd made a point of not getting involved with any men since Jared's death, and for good reason. Men were nothing but trouble, especially the drop-dead gorgeous, steal-your-breath sexy ones.

She knew better now. Even the sexy ones couldn't break down her defenses.

But Penn? He was on the inside before her defenses were up—always had been.

An ache built in her chest as he just stood there, as if he was waiting for something.

"I don't know what you want me to say," she said finally. "I don't even know what *this* is."

That hadn't been a question; but the dark look in his eyes gave just enough of a warning that she could have shoved him away and run if she'd been so inclined. But, oh yes, she was insane, because she stayed right where she was, let the world turn into a blur…and let him close those inches of space between his lips and hers, let him slide his hand behind her neck into the damp tendrils of her hair, and kiss her.

It wasn't an innocent kiss. It was hard and deep and sexy. She could feel his body against hers, in all the right places, could feel his heat, his urgency, his soul-wrenching need to taste her. She felt her control snap, her reservations slip away, as she responded to him.

She felt…drunk.

Then it was over and he was staring down into her eyes, his breaths coming in soft jerks, just like her own. Her pulse was speeding madly and she had a wild, reckless urge to push him back on the kitchen table and jump on top of him.

She was, quite clearly, insane. Just like he was.

"We can't—no more—that's it." She stumbled all over what words she could get out. Humiliating, that's what *this* was. Tears sprang to her eyes. Not because she was embarrassed, but because now she'd had it rammed home just what she'd lost all those years ago, and—no matter what Penn was thinking— what could not be brought back. "We can't do this!"

"We just did," he said calmly.

Calmly.

Damn him.

Only, she'd seen how he was affected, too. How his breath had caught, how his body had gone hard, how his eyes burned hot.

But that didn't matter. So what if he wanted her? That didn't solve all of life's problems. And just because she'd never felt this kind of fire with anyone else…

That didn't matter, either. Passion wasn't everything.

And, wow, that threw some cold water on her. In fact, it made her feel dead inside, when she'd just felt more alive than she could remember feeling in a long, long time.

"Well, we can't do it again!" Now she did what she should have done before, shoved at him. He rocked back a step and she pushed around him. Where she was going, she had no idea.

"You're running, Willa."

She wheeled. "Whatever!"

"Why are you so upset?"

She didn't know what to say to that. Then she came up with something.

"This isn't a game! We aren't kids who don't have to think about the past and the present and the future! I have a little girl upstairs. I have a life here. I can't afford to play around. I have work to do. I have to keep my head on straight. This isn't going anywhere between the two of us. You're going back to New York."

"And is that the only reason this can't happen, Willa? Because I'm going back to New York?"

"No, it's not the only reason," she charged on, confused and not liking it. "I don't believe you that you don't care about the past. How's that?"

She shouldn't have brought that up. She was sorry, instantly.

"You're right, I care about the past." He stepped toward her, closing the gap again. The light from the candle on the table flickered on his face, made his eyes seem darker and brighter at the same time. "But I want to let it go. You have to let it go, too."

She blew out a suddenly angry breath. "You're so

self-righteous! I guess I should be grateful you want to forgive me!"

"Would you like it better if I didn't?"

"Maybe!"

"Okay. I don't forgive you. It was all your fault and you were totally responsible for ruining what we could have had. You made a huge mistake and your life will never be the same. You're a terrible person. What else do you want to hear, Willa?"

She knew, on some level, that that was a ploy, that he didn't mean it, that he was just trying to snap her out of her own self-judgment, her own inability to accept his forgiveness. But he didn't know, couldn't know, how sharp his words stung.

How right on target they were.

How they devastated her.

She couldn't breathe, all of a sudden, she hurt so much.

"Willa—"

She knew, on the fringes of her blind pain, that he had realized that his words hadn't worked their intended magic.

"Willa." He was there, reaching for her.

She pushed him away, wheeled, ran for the stairs and nearly knocked Birdie down.

"Mommy? What's wrong, Mommy?"

Oh, God, she didn't want Birdie to see her completely, hysterically falling apart.

"Are you okay?" She blinked through the blur of

tears, steadied Birdie. "Go get a cookie." Did they have cookies? She couldn't even remember. "I'll…I'll be right back."

She had to get to her bedroom. She made it, slammed the door, slid down the door to the floor, trying to sob as silently as possible.

Seeing Penn again…

Kissing Penn again…

It brought it all up so vividly. Not that it had ever gone away. It was there all the time, this deep, dark secret, like a cancer eating away at her life. Had she really believed she could lie it away?

New York City wasn't the only thing that stood between them. It was her terrible lie that made the biggest barrier of all.

She swiped angrily at her eyes, rubbing at the tears, willing them to stop. What did she think she was going to do about it now?

Tell Penn the truth?

She put her palms on the floor and pushed herself to her feet. She had to stop thinking about it. She was scaring the crap out of herself. She went into the bathroom, splashed her face with cold water. *Pull it together,* she told herself.

Downstairs, she found Birdie sitting on the sofa in the parlor, snuggled up to Penn. He looked up as she came down the stairs, his expression disarmingly awkward, as if he had no idea what he was doing reading to a four-year-old, and yet he looked right at home at the same time. She knew through Otto that Penn had never married, but she had no doubt he'd make a great father someday. He was sweet and caring and playful, even as he was hot and edgy and dangerous.

She steeled herself against the emotions that threatened to charge back.

"Join us?" Penn said.

"Come on, Mama!" Birdie begged. She scooted off the couch and ran to the corner of the room, grabbing a long box. "I want to play Candyland."

"I'm going to see about starting something for dinner," Willa said.

Anything. She'd do anything rather than sit down with Penn and Birdie when she was feeling this emotional.

It was rainy and dark outside. She'd push up dinner, then push up bedtime. Next thing she knew, it'd be tomorrow, at that rate.

There was an old bottle of elderberry wine in the cupboard. Alone in the kitchen, she poured herself a glass. She wasn't much of a drinker; the wine had been a gift to Otto.

She wondered how much elderberry wine it would take to get drunk.

After she took the first sip, she wondered if she'd learned anything in fourteen years about how much of a brain she had after she'd been drinking. She poured the rest of the glass down the sink.

She could hear Birdie giggling in the other room, the muted wind and rain wrapping around the house, the sound of her own pulse pounding in her ears. She was going to go stark-raving mad, trapped in this old farmhouse with Penn.

Trapped in this farmhouse or trapped in her lies? Trapped in her *life?*

She really could have used that elderberry wine. And one glass wouldn't hurt.

Willa poured a glass again, and this time headed out the back, surprised to find the door locked. She didn't usually lock doors out here, and she knew she hadn't locked any of them after they came in from the barn. Weird that Penn would lock it. He was from the city now, though.

The small porch out there had a rocking chair. Usually, she liked to sit and watch the rain. She'd drink her coffee out there most mornings.

This rain was different. Noah's Ark proportions, for one thing. Incredibly dark for another. It had been like twilight all day.

She sat in the rocker, sipped the sweet wine, and looked for her horse, trying to differentiate an equine shape among the shadows of the trees. The barn hadn't burned completely before the rain put it out, but the dark outline of its shell was a depressing reminder. There was a smaller barn in the meadow down the hill.

Black Beauty might even be down there already, she

supposed. She certainly wasn't going to go look. She'd had it with this rain. And the horse, unlike the cows, was smart enough to stay safe and close to home.

She thought she saw something move through the trees. Had Beauty come back on her own? She stood up, walked to the edge of the porch, one hand holding her glass, the other arm wrapping around her middle in the chill dampness under the roofed porch.

"Willa."

She hadn't heard the door. She turned, too quickly, and some of the wine sloshed out of her too-full glass. She *really* wasn't meant to have this wine.

"It's cold out here," Penn said. "Why don't you come inside?"

"Is something wrong?"

He didn't say anything for too long. "We miss you in there."

Her pulse started to throb. She couldn't go in there and make a little domestic tableau with him and Birdie. It hurt too much.

"Please."

He said the one word simply, but somehow so grimly that she was nervous in a whole different way.

"You're freaking me out," she said. "Is there something you're not telling me?"

She darted a glance over her shoulder, almost expecting to see a bogeyman behind her.

Nothing. Just trees and darkness. Wind and rain.

Birdie appeared, poking her head out the door.

"I beat him at Candyland!" she told Willa, then threw her arms around Penn's waist. "Will you carry me? Please, please, please!"

Willa moved her gaze back to Penn, searching his face. Unreadable, that's what he was now.

Birdie was trying to climb on his back. Jeez, she had a lot of energy; and Penn was a good sport. But even as he bent down to let Birdie climb on, the expression in his eyes stayed the same. Grim.

She remembered how he'd gone out to look at her tires in the rain, claiming that they'd been flattened. Then there'd been that fire at the barn.

A rush of nerves swept her. She searched his face, his so grim, do-what-I-say eyes.

No, she had to be imagining any sinister meaning behind his insistence that she go back inside. Her imagination was off the charts, that's all.

Next, Birdie would be telling her the *house* wanted her inside.

Just the same, she suddenly had no urge to remain on the back porch alone. Even if it meant her only other option was going inside with Penn.

Chapter 12

Penn didn't want to scare Willa. In truth, he had no concrete reason to believe anything strange was going on. But the possibility skirted around the back of his mind and wouldn't go away.

"I need to talk to you," he said. He glanced pointedly at Birdie. "Later."

Willa's face showed confusion, a little fear, and he wasn't sure what she was thinking, if he wanted to talk to her about why he'd insisted she come inside, or about their conversation earlier. She let it drop, though, and started grilling cheese sandwiches in a sandwich press, while Birdie sat on Penn's lap in the kitchen, drawing in her coloring book with her crayons, on the big, scarred kitchen table, and keeping up a monologue that didn't seem to require much participation on anyone else's part.

"She talks a lot," Willa remarked. She set plates on the table and started bringing grilled sandwiches over.

"I noticed," Penn said.

"She doesn't usually have anyone to talk to but me," Willa added. "She's excited about you being here."

He wished Willa talked as freely. Something had upset her earlier, above and beyond his words. He hadn't meant her to take them seriously. He suspected she knew that, but they had triggered something he hadn't intended.

"You're a good mother, Willa," he said.

She looked uncomfortable. "I try. I'm certainly not perfect."

"You don't have to be perfect. Don't be so hard on yourself."

That prickly exterior, and all that beauty, covered a fragile woman with lousy self-esteem. It was something he'd never thought about when they were kids, but he could see it now.

She went on about dinner and he didn't force the conversation. It felt as if she was rushing the evening. Fixing dinner. Pushing plates on them. Next, she'd be shooing them off to bed.

He didn't want to be shooed. He had questions, and he wanted answers. And tonight could be his last chance. The storm had to let up sometime. Work crews would get the phone lines repaired. Road crews would get the roads open. Willa would be calling a tow truck out here to haul off his vehicle and him with it, dropping him off at the 1950s-era, one-story roadhouse motel outside town.

True to his expectations, no sooner had they finished their sandwiches than she was setting water to boil for hot chocolate for Birdie's bedtime treat.

"We need to go to bed early tonight, peeps," she told Birdie. "We don't want to run the generator any more than we have to. We don't know if we'll have the power back tomorrow or not."

"We can light more candles!" Birdie suggested.

"We'll run out of candles before we know it," Willa told her.

Penn watched Willa fix Birdie's hot chocolate.

"Do I have to go to bed, too?" he joked.

"That's up to you." She poured a cup of hot chocolate, then turned and said, "Come on, Birdie. I'll bring your hot chocolate. Grab your bear and we'll read books."

Run away, run away. That's what she was doing, and he was helpless to stop her.

"We still need to talk," he said. "It's important."

She nodded, but he didn't know if she'd come back down. She left, taking Birdie with her, the little girl still arguing that she wanted to stay up, that she wanted to play Go Fish, that she wanted another sandwich.

Penn sat there in the flicker of the one candle left

lit in the kitchen, feeling oddly alone. He could remember sitting right here in this kitchen when he was a kid, as far back as when his grandmother was still alive—could remember her baking pies in her apron. She was never without her apron, and she seemed to be able to come up with anything out of its deep pockets. She was always bringing in food from the big garden she had, canning, and storing up for winter in the cellar. While his own parents had lived in a house in town—his father had worked in the insurance business—he'd spent as much time out here at Limberlost as he had in town, it seemed.

Or maybe it was just how it was in his memory. The hours he'd spent at Limberlost stood out, seemed more real, all these years later.

He got up and walked around the house, checking all the doors, making sure everything was locked up tight. He didn't know what else he could do at this point.

It was hard to believe anyone could be out there intending them harm, though he still wanted to talk to Willa about it. For the life of him, he couldn't think of anyone who could be interested in this farm but Marcus and Jess, and he didn't like how uncomfortable Willa had been discussing Marcus. It nagged at his gut.

He'd been away a long time, but Willa had been here all the while. She knew more about his family than he did, and he needed to find out what she knew.

Walking back into the old kitchen, he sat down at the table, the past and the present seeming like one in the enfolding night and sudden quiet. He realized the storm outside had died down.

He almost felt as if he could look up and he would see Otto there. He'd been a hardworking man, just as Penn's father had been, and as was Penn.

He'd watched his grandparents work the farm, and he had thought there had to be an easier way to make a living. He'd watched his father struggle to operate a business in a small town, and had thought there had to be a better place to get rich.

And he'd done pretty well by himself in New York—was on the verge of doing even better. He was ready for his own firm, with clients that would follow him from Brown and Sons.

In New York he lived alone, had lived alone for years, without feeling alone. Maybe there was something about being back in Haven, back where he'd once been surrounded by family and friends. Now there was just the farm, and cousins he no longer had contact with. And Willa and Birdie in this house.

Dammit, he had his whole life in the bustling, never-alone city, where he had his work to keep him company and fill his every waking—and sometimes sleeping—moments. It shook him to realize that he'd barely thought about his work since he'd come to Haven. He'd put in his resignation at the firm already, in anticipation of living out his month's requirement at Limberlost, then getting the property sold and digging straight into the work of opening up his own firm.

Penn was, in fact, up a creek if Willa's version of the will held up.

He'd have no job and no money to start up his own firm. What would he do then? His whole life had been fixed so narrowly for so long, the thought of doing something else seemed impossible. As he watched the dying candle sputter and go dark, he thought that the last twenty-four hours had been like a meteor colliding with his destined life course.

Or was it his life finally colliding with his destiny?

Willa read through all three of the story books twice, then Birdie had to talk about the chickens they were going to get. They were ordering eggs to hatch, and Willa had already bought the incubator. Birdie wanted to name them Petunia, Daffodil and Porky. Willa didn't know why she thought there were just going to be three, but decided not to tell Birdie she was ordering two dozen, because she was already off naming their yet-to-be-purchased goats.

And Willa hoped they could really get the chickens and goats, that Otto had done what he promised, that they were still going to be living on this farm.

She read through the story books for a third time and finally Birdie fell asleep. She sat by the side of the bed and watched her daughter, listening to her quiet breathing. There was nothing more difficult for her to imagine than if she had to move Birdie away from Limberlost.

Determined not to start crying about it, she got up, splashed cold water on her face in the bathroom and brushed her teeth. Penn thought she was a good mother and it was pathetic that that had almost made her cry when he told her.

Tell Penn the truth.

She was so tired of all the lies. There was a way out….

If she was as brave as she hoped she was teaching Birdie to be.

Her knees were shaking when she kissed Birdie good-night, and left the room.

In the hall, she shut the door softly and looked down the stairs. It was dark. She'd taken ages with Birdie. Maybe Penn had given up and gone to bed.

She took a candle with her and went down the stairs anyway. The stairs were dark and quiet. Had the storm quit? She didn't hear anything from outside now, though it was pitch-black out the big parlor windows as she walked into the kitchen. It was dark there, too.

"Hey."

She almost dropped the candle. She pivoted, looked for Penn. He was sitting at the table. In the dark.

Just sitting there.

"What are you doing?" she blurted.

"Thinking."

"In the dark?"

"You can think in any kind of light, Willa."

She felt a beat of frustration in her stomach. She wasn't up to conversational gymnastics. She wasn't sure she was up to being as brave as she wanted to teach Birdie to be, after all.

"Is this where I'm supposed to ask you what you're thinking about?" Because she wouldn't—at all. Heading straight back upstairs, that was her. And she started to do just that.

"About you," he answered.

"I didn't ask," she said without turning around. But she stopped.

What was wrong with her?

She started walking away again. *'Fraidy cat.*

"Wait."

No, don't wait, she told herself. But she did; she couldn't help it. He was thinking about her, he'd said that. He was making her so nervous, she should be *running* up the stairs. If she waited, he was going to keep on, and tell her exactly what he'd been thinking about her.

And she knew, even before he told her, that she'd be better off not hearing it.

"I wanted a chance to apologize for upsetting you," he said slowly. "I didn't mean what I said. I was trying to get you to realize you were being bull-headed, that's all. It wasn't the right way for me to go about it. I'm sorry, Willa."

She bit her lip in the dark, turned back. All the way across the room, she couldn't see anything of him but the shadow of his big, muscular shoulders and the shine of his eyes.

It was suddenly way, way too quiet.

"I'm oversensitive sometimes," she said.

"Sometimes I'm an ass."

She hadn't expected that, or that he could make her laugh in this moment. This moment where he was blowing her mind because he kept caring about how she felt. She'd never known anyone to care this much about how she felt. She was used to pushing her feelings aside, minimizing them.

The important people in her life had minimized her feelings. All except Penn.

He acted like *how she felt* was so important to him.

"Am I supposed to agree, or argue?" she asked finally.

"What do you want to do?"

Jump in your lap, was the first thing that sprang to her wayward mind. There was no denying it. She was terribly, atrociously, ridiculously sexually attracted to him. She might as well face that and get past it.

She couldn't even blame that on positive ions, no matter how wild she stretched her imagination. Who wouldn't be attracted to a good-looking man like Penn? She was only human.

"I want to go back to bed." Yeah, that would be the smart thing. What was she doing, waiting for his permission? This was where she was supposed to say something rude or confrontational, create conflict to put distance between them, then run and hide.

"Can you answer me one question first?" he asked quietly.

She swallowed nervously.

"Okay."

"I've been sitting here thinking," he said slowly, "about a lot of things. You're right, it's been a long time. Maybe it's being back in Haven again. Maybe it's Otto being gone. I wanted out of Haven all my life, that's true, but I guess I always felt like a part of me was here as long as Granddad was here. It's strange, knowing he's gone. You're a…connection to the past. If nothing else, I hope we can be friends again, Willa."

Friends. He wanted to be friends.

Well. Wasn't that just a sick thud in her stomach? But she should be happy. Relieved. He was talking sense now.

"I didn't mean to come off like an arrogant jerk, telling you that I forgave you for what happened back then," he went on. "I just don't think it's something that needs to stand between us now. It was a long time ago. We were kids, really, even if we thought we were so grown up. You know, if Birdie was eighteen, you'd look at her and think she was still a kid."

Yeah, she would, she knew that. Eighteen wasn't nearly as big and bad as you thought it was when you were actually that age.

"I know," she said.

"Everything happened so fast. I came back from that trip and…"

And she was pregnant. She wouldn't answer his phone calls. She wouldn't see him. But he managed to find her outside the house one day. No one was home, just her, and he wouldn't take no for an answer when she tried to walk away.

Not until she told him that she was pregnant and that the baby wasn't his. Because there was no way, *no way,* she could lie to him about *that,* try to pretend it was his.

No matter what else she lied to him about.

She wouldn't tell him whose baby it was. But she knew he made his own call when she married Jared. By then, he was already out of town, off to college.

As hard as he'd tried to talk to her, the conversation, when it happened, was short and bitter.

"I guess it feels like unfinished business," he said.

"Are you saying you want closure?" She didn't know what he wanted. She didn't know what *she* wanted. He had her off-balance all the time.

"If we're going to have any chance at all of starting over, Willa, we've got to put the past behind us." He stood, and her pulse skipped wildly as he stepped slowly toward her. "Do you think we can do that?"

As he drew nearer, the flickering candle she held cast light across his intense features, but it was his eyes that took her breath away. There was a ghost of vulnerability lurking in the dark heat of them. A vulnerability she'd last seen that day at her house, right before she'd told him she was pregnant. He'd shut down seconds later, then he was gone.

She avoided his question.

"Starting over?" Her heart thumped. "I thought you just said you wanted to be friends."

"I was trying not to scare you too much."

He was terrifying her.

"Okay, well…" Her throat clogged up. "It's not that easy for me. Putting the past behind me." The past was always with her. She carried it on her shoulders. There could be no starting over, not without telling Penn the truth.

And she had no idea how she thought she would be able to do that.

"We can't start over," she said firmly. That was that. She couldn't do it.

"Tell me what you're afraid of, Willa."

He was right in front of her, the heat in his eyes incinerating her. And oh, he was right, she was so scared. Penn had been her safety, once upon a time.

He wasn't saying a word now, just looking at her in a way that had her head spinning. She set her candle down on the kitchen counter for fear she'd drop it.

"I'm scared of lots of things. Where do you want me to start? I'm scared that you're acting like you think there's a bogeyman in the woods—locking doors, telling me to stay inside."

That was all true, of course, but she knew better than to think that was the answer he'd been seeking.

"Yes, I am scared there could be someone out there," he admitted grimly, surprising her. "I don't know who or why, but it's possible."

"Where would they hide out? The barns? The barn up here is gone now." The barn in the meadow was small, and open on both sides. "There's an old pump house on the hill." That was little more than a shack. And the idea made no sense. "Why would anyone want to do that, hide out here, try to harm us?"

"I don't know, Willa. I don't know that it was a bear that attacked me. I don't know if it was lightning that burned that barn down. I don't know what happened to your tires. I don't know why I got an anonymous text message warning me not to come back to West Virginia."

"What?"

"I got an anonymous message warning me not to come," he repeated. "I even wondered, when I first got here, if it might have been you."

"It wasn't me!"

"I know that. I said, when I first got here."

There was a heavy beat of quiet.

"Maybe it's the earthquake." She felt a bubble of hysteria rising in her throat. "Anything can happen in Haven." *Maybe it was the house!*

Now she was losing it.

"Do you have any enemies, Willa?"

"No! Are you *trying* to scare me?"

"I don't want to scare you."

"Then stop it! Look, the storm's stopped. We'll get the phones back tomorrow and we'll call for help, get you out of here." Then it would be over, at least the part where she was trapped in this house with him.

"I don't want to leave you alone here, Willa."

She didn't want to think he was manipulating her, scaring her so that she would depend on him. So he could have that second chance he had no way of knowing was impossible. But there were only two options. He was either trying to scare her for his own reasons, or he really believed there was some kind of danger on the farm.

"I think you're hiding something," he went on. "I don't know why, but I want you to tell me, whatever it is."

"I don't have any enemies, if that's what you want to know!"

He shook his head. "What about Marcus?"

She felt the blood drain from her face. "What about him?"

"Why are you shaking, Willa? Why does it upset you to talk about him?"

"Why are you asking me these questions?"

"Because, if anyone wants this farm and therefore wants to get rid of you and me, it makes sense that it's one of my cousins."

Her pulse thudded.

"That sounds crazy!"

"Maybe it is. But there's something you're not telling me about Marcus, and I want to know what it is. If you won't tell me, as soon as this is over and I can get out of here, I'm going to Marcus. I'll ask him why you turn white as a sheet when his name is mentioned."

"Well, he won't tell you!"

Oh, God!

Her head reeled. Penn closed what was left of the gap between them, grabbed her by both arms before she could run.

"So there *is* something you're not telling me."

"I didn't say that." She'd screwed up and she couldn't think straight, not with him so close, not with the way he was scaring her with all this talk about someone out to do them harm.

Penn's gaze pinned her, fierce and hot. "Tell me what it is, Willa. Tell me what you're hiding."

In the dead still of the night there came a rattling sound from the front of the house. Then pounding.

"Someone's at the door," Willa whispered harshly.

"Don't move." Penn dropped his hold, and strode out of the kitchen.

Willa went right after him. No way was she staying in the kitchen alone. Suddenly, she didn't want to be anywhere alone. Her head was reeling and she wanted to climb right into Penn's arms.

And that he was her safety, again, was just as head reeling as everything else.

Her name was yelled from the other side of the door. "Willa!"

She stopped dead in the front hall behind Penn.

"It's Marcus," she breathed.

Fear thumped in her veins. Marcus was here, on the farm.

Had Marcus been hiding out at Limberlost? Was he responsible for all the incidents? Thoughts raced wildly through her head, nothing making sense.

She pushed past Penn, flipped on the porch light, praying the generator still had power. Even as Penn's arms wrapped around her, as if he feared she'd open the door, she pressed her eye to the peephole in the old door. Marcus stood there in the light. He looked awful, haggard, drenched and dirty. She hadn't seen him in years, and he looked every bit the frightening monster.

Her throat clogged with dread at what he held in his hand.

Marcus banged on the door, shouting for her to open up.

Penn was already pushing her aside to look.

He turned back to her. In the dark, she could see only the grim determination in his eyes.

"Move," he said, grabbing her, pulling her away from the door, into the hall between the front room and the kitchen. "He could shoot right through that door."

She hadn't even thought of that. They were both lucky they weren't dead right now.

"Where is Otto's shotgun?" he asked her.

"Open the door or everybody'll be dead, Willa!" Marcus was shouting now. His words sounded slurred, wild. "Want that little girl of yours to die?"

Willa's heart banged in her chest. "He's crazy or drunk—or both," she whispered.

"Where's Otto's shotgun?" Penn repeated.

"There's a locked box in the back of the closet. There's another one in the pantry with the bullets."

"Where's the key?"

"I'll get it." She ran, first to the pantry to grab the box with the bullets, then to her purse for the keys, then back to Penn in the hall. He'd already pulled the box from the closet. She fumbled with the lock on the box of bullets.

Penn took it from her, unlocked it, emptied out bullets, then broke open the gun and started loading.

"Willa!" The banging went on and on.

Any minute, Birdie would wake up and be terrified, she just knew it.

"You want to leave me out here to die, Willa?" Marcus shouted. "You want me to pay?" There was a cracking thud on the door.

"Oh my God, he's going to break the door down," she said thinly.

"He's not going to hurt you, Willa," Penn promised.

He had the shotgun loaded.

Willa could barely think over the blood pounding in her ears. Marcus was insane, completely insane.

"Everybody's gonna die, Willa!" Marcus shouted. "Not just me!"

There was another cracking thud on the door.

"Go upstairs, Willa," Penn ordered. "Go to Birdie. Make sure she's okay."

She didn't want to leave Penn.

"What about you?"

What was he planning to do? What if he opened that door and Marcus shot him?

"I'm going to talk to Marcus."

"Are you going to shoot him?"

"I don't want to."

Oh, God. He would, if he had to. Marcus was crazy, drunk, or both, but he was still Penn's cousin. And Penn was going to try to talk to him.

The sound that exploded from the front porch was deafening, or maybe that was just the utter, awful silence that followed.

Chapter 13

"What happened?" Willa whispered thinly, finally.

"Stay here." Penn moved quickly, a shadow in the shadows, toward the front door.

Willa's pulse thunked wildly. That had been a gunshot!

There was no more shouting. Nothing. Total silence. Frightening, deadly silence.

Penn came back. "Go upstairs," he ordered.

"Why? What's going on?"

"Go upstairs, Willa."

Fear and dread had her brain swimming. "What happened?" she insisted wildly.

Penn was nothing but a solid shape before her in the dark hall, a hard gleam revealing his eyes.

"Marcus is dead. He shot himself in the head."

"Oh, my God." She stumbled backward, hit the wall, her head reeling all over again. "What are you going to do?"

"I'm going to get something to cover him. We can't leave him there like that. What if Birdie saw him? We can't move him. We have to wait for the police."

They couldn't call the police, not until the phones came back.

"Are you sure he's dead?" She was still terrified.

"He shot himself in the *head*," Penn said. "He's dead."

"I think there is an old tarp in there," Willa told him. "It's folded up. I know where it is." The cellar, once separate from the old farmhouse, had been enclosed when a laundry room had been added to the house.

She couldn't believe she was having this conversation, with Marcus dead on the porch.

The silence was suddenly broken by wind whipping up, creaking around the sides of the house, then a pounding on the roof.

She knew that sound. "It's hailing again."

The storm from hell wasn't through yet.

"I need a plastic baggie, a large one, and a towel," Penn said.

"Why?"

"I'm not leaving a gun laying there with a small child around."

"You know we're not supposed to touch it," Willa said.

"I don't care."

She swallowed hard. Okay. She didn't care, either. He was right. It was too big a risk. She found a plastic bag and a towel.

Penn was already heading for the cellar. Willa went to the kitchen, blew out the candle, and started turning on lights, saving the generator power be damned. Her knees felt like melted jelly. He'd already found the tarp by the time she got the baggie and towel, and she went with him to the front door.

She made the mistake of looking when he opened it. Marcus lay sprawled backward, blood on the porch rails where he must have hit and slid down.

His face was unrecognizable.

She turned away quickly, sickness rising in her throat.

The wind howled and hail rained down on the porch roof, adding its clatter to the horror. She forced herself to take deep breaths, and by the time she turned back, Penn had him covered.

She handed him the bag and the towel.

When he stood, she could see the desperation in his own eyes. This was his cousin. They hadn't been close for years, but this was agony to Penn, just the same.

Back inside, all the lights were on around them, the night black against the windows. The hail had turned to rain. She watched Penn put away the gun.

She locked up the handgun he'd taken from the porch, along with the shotgun.

She couldn't believe what had just happened, her mind refusing to wrap completely around it. Penn found her in the kitchen. His face revealed haggard exhaustion.

"Why?" She felt that bubble of hysteria rising up again in her throat. "What was he doing here? Why would he threaten to kill me and Birdie—then kill himself?"

"That's what I want to know."

She swallowed thickly. "I heard he was sick. Maybe it was mental illness. Maybe he was a drunk." Maybe that's why he didn't show up for Otto's funeral.

"I didn't see a car out there, and there's no way he could have gotten here tonight. He's been hiding out on the farm. Maybe he slashed your tires. Maybe he attacked me at the creek. Maybe he burned the barn down. Why?"

"I don't know."

Suddenly Penn was right in front of her. He grabbed her shoulders. "You know something, Willa."

"Maybe he wants the farm," she tried desperately. "Maybe he doesn't think it's fair for either you or I to have it. Maybe he wants everything for himself. He wanted us all dead. Oh my God, what if he's killed Jess already?"

"I don't think he was after the farm," Penn said. "He was after you, Willa."

"You were attacked down by the creek."

"Maybe he didn't want me around. Wherever he was hiding out, maybe he had alcohol and he got drunk. He was suicidal, Willa. How many stories do you see on the news of people who go after someone and end up shooting themselves? Sometimes they take other people with them. This time, it didn't go down that way. Was Marcus in love with you?"

She froze completely. "No!"

The pain in his eyes was almost palpable, stabbing straight into her heart.

"My cousin just shot himself outside this house," he rasped. "Shot himself, calling for you, trying to get to you. If there is something you're hiding, you have to tell it to me now."

"I don't know what it could have to do with anything," she cried. "It's in the past. I don't know why he would come here now, what he wanted with me."

His gaze shone with desperation. "What did he want with you in the past?"

"Don't make me tell you." She was so scared. What was the point of the truth now? Marcus was dead.

"I need to know."

And, oh God, his voice broke. Emotion choked her throat. She was shaking so hard. She lifted her hands and covered her face.

"I wasn't pregnant with Jared's baby," she whispered.

There was only the sound of the storm and the hard thud of her pulse for an awful beat.

"What do you mean, Willa?"

She dropped her eyes, met his terrible gaze. "When we broke up, that wasn't Jared's baby. It was Marcus's."

"What?"

Penn dropped his hold on her, stepped back. Shock tore across his eyes. She felt sick regret already.

"I shouldn't have told you. I knew I shouldn't have told you. You don't have to believe me. I never said anything. Nobody knew what happened. It doesn't matter. It's too late!"

"What happened?"

His emotions were so raw, she couldn't read them. Pain, yes, maybe disgust, too. She didn't know.

He had hold of her arms again then. "What happened?" he repeated louder.

It was a miracle Birdie hadn't woken through all of this.

"You slept with my *cousin?*" he went on.

"He—"

"What, Willa? He what?"

"He raped me."

Penn's expression was murderous.

"I was down at the river one day. He came down there. We were just playing around, swimming, talking." The words poured out, her voice thick and trembling. "He had beer. I had a couple. I shouldn't have. I don't even like beer! Then he said I was teasing him, flaunting myself in my little bikini, and then—" Her heart sank. Penn was looking at her like she was the most horrible creature in the world. She thought she was going to throw up. "I'm sorry. Just forget it. I didn't want to tell you. I knew it would make things worse. I knew you wouldn't believe me. And now he's dead. It's not like you can ask him about it. There's no reason for you to believe me."

She pushed away from him, ripping from his hold.

"I didn't want to tell you," she whispered thinly again, turned, and ran to the stairs.

He was after her before she knew it. She stumbled at the foot of the stairs and he caught her in his arms. They fell together, him blocking the brunt of the hit with his body.

He cradled her in his arms. "Willa, Willa."

She heard the thickness of his voice and realized he was crying. Big, strong Penn Ramsey, crying. It devastated her.

"You don't know how I feel," he said shakily, fiercely. "You don't know what I believe. Will you give me a chance? Please?"

She looked up at him, felt his heart pounding as hers was, saw the hot rawness of his fierce, moist gaze.

"For once, give me a chance, Willa."

"I don't know how," she admitted.

"You didn't tell me. You let me think you betrayed me. You let me think Jared was the father when you married him." His voice wasn't accusing, just…confused and hurt.

She hated that hurt, hated knowing she'd caused it. Misery knifed her.

"He was your cousin," she whispered. "I didn't want to hurt you. I didn't think anyone would believe me."

His dark, liquid eyes burned into her. "Why? You knew that I loved you. You knew that I would have done anything for you."

Past tense. Of course. Even at that, it nearly killed her to hear it.

"I don't think—" She couldn't complete the words.

"You didn't believe *me*," he said roughly. "Why, Willa? You didn't believe me then, and you don't believe me now. Maybe you don't ever believe anyone. Is that why you married Jared, stayed with him, even when it was awful? You'd rather have something you know you can't believe in than something you just might believe—that's too scary for you?"

Oh, God. He knew her so well, saw through her so easily.

"You didn't love Jared," he said.

No. She hadn't loved Birdie's father, as horrible as that was. Not in the deep, passionate, real way she'd loved Penn.

"Why, Willa?"

She knew that question covered so much ground—and it was dark, painful, horrible ground. Penn deserved an answer. She owed him the rest of the truth.

"When I was ten, my stepfather started noticing me." Her chest was tight, and she could barely choke the words out, her voice shaking and thin. "He raped me when I was twelve. It went on for a while." She felt the sudden tightness of Penn's grip around her, felt the almost edgy pulse of his arms around her. She had the sudden sense that if he could get his hands on her stepfather right now, he would kill him, and that scared her and touched her at the same time. "It stopped when I was thirteen," she whispered. "I think my mother knew. She must have done something, I don't really know, but it stopped. No one ever spoke of it—not my mother, not me. You didn't talk about things like that in my house. My stepfather told me it was my fault, that I tempted him. Marcus said the same thing. I did blame myself. I drank the beer—"

"That didn't give him a right to rape you, Willa."

His hold was so fierce, his voice so intense.

"I didn't talk about it. I didn't know how to talk about it. I didn't think anyone would believe me. I thought it was my fault."

"You still think it's your fault."

He made the statement simply, flatly.

"Maybe," she choked out.

"It was not!" He took hold of her face, tenderly, sweetly. "It was not your fault. I wish you had told me, but I can't blame you for that, either. I know why you didn't. I want you to believe in yourself."

"I'm trying."

Looking at him hurt, but she couldn't stop. He still touched her, so lightly, skimming his fingertips along her jaw and up behind her ear, to the back of her neck, twining his fingers in her hair. And she couldn't, absolutely couldn't, run away anymore. The truth was, she didn't want to run.

Her heart felt tight, achy. And he just held her there, studying her, as if he might study her forever, while her pulse thumped and she could barely breathe.

"I want you to believe in me, too," he said. "Will you try?"

Wind shook the house and rain beat down outside.

"Will you just hold me," she whispered, "and tell me that everything will be all right?"

Chapter 14

Penn knew Willa was scared. Hell, *he* was scared. All he could do was be honest with her, completely honest, as honest as she had finally been with him. And there was nothing more honest when she lifted her face to his than to kiss her.

Her lips were so soft, so sweet, her body so warm and so familiar. She lifted one arm and put it around his neck and kissed him back, opened her mouth and shockingly invited him in. He took it slow, easy, to give her time to back out if she wanted to. But she didn't. She kept on kissing him right back.

He pulled away slowly, to look into her eyes. The liquid pain in them stung him. There was so much pain inside Willa. She'd always been a bit of a mystery, even when they were kids. There was always something secret about Willa. He had wanted to know her completely, and he was filled with a deep gratitude that she had finally opened up to him. That was terrifying for her, he knew that.

In the midst of this storm, with death at their very door, this was life. He and Willa.

She licked her lips nervously, as if unsure of his intentions. Or maybe sure, and that's why she was nervous. But she wasn't running.

She could, if she wanted to. But he hoped with every fiber of his being that she wouldn't. In the midst of death, they had life, and he needed to feel that life, feel it with her. Then, maybe then, he could convince himself as much as her that everything really would be all right.

He held her gaze for a long, long moment. The steady throb of her nearness pounded in his veins.

"I missed you, Willa," he said. He could hear the rough, raspy need in his voice that shocked even him. He'd been full of hurt and pride when he'd turned his back on her. But now he was baring himself—just like she'd bared herself to him. "You don't know how hard that is to admit."

Her mouth trembled in response, and he felt like he was shaking in his boots. He didn't want to be rejected by her again. Not now, not when he needed her so much.

She gave a half sob, half laugh, and said, "Yes, I do."

"I don't want you to think I'm trying to take a turn in your bed, as if I think you sleep with men all the time. I don't want you to think I don't respect you. It's nothing like that. I just..." He shook his head. There were no words other than the humble truth. "I respect you. More than you probably believe. I just need to feel alive right now. And you make me feel that way."

"I don't think any of that," she whispered. "I know better, with you."

That was a big admission.

He held her soft, wet gaze. She was crying a little bit, he saw now. One tear escaped to track down her cheek. He reached up, thumbed it away, kept his palm there, cradling her face.

"Then, what are you thinking?" He had to know.

"You make me feel alive, too," she answered.

He didn't know what he wanted to hear, but it was enough. It was a confession, at the least, that he was important to her. And it floored him.

Softly, he kissed her again, loving the taste of her, loving the way she responded to him. She made a moaning sound in her throat and he left her lips to kiss her neck, letting his hands roam down her waist, her hips, wanting—needing—to know every part of her. To remember every part of her. He was desperate for her, not just with his body but with his heart, his soul.

It was as if he'd never left. All the bitterness and sarcasm that had festered as an adult fell away. With

Willa, he could feel the innocence, the hope, he'd just about forgotten.

He didn't want to let go of that feeling, or of Willa.

"You are so beautiful to me," he whispered in her ear as he drew his tongue up her neck to her face again. He nibbled on her delicate earlobe and she shivered in his arms.

He didn't know what tomorrow would hold, what would become of everything when the will was settled.

But he wanted to stamp her heart with this night, so that she wouldn't forget it. So that, no matter what happened, she would still give them whatever second chance Fate had made possible here.

He looked at her again now. She *was* so beautiful. He saw in her still-moist eyes all the intensity, all the tumbled feelings; he recognized because he felt them, too. Hope, fear, need. And pain, he saw pain, too.

"I want to go to your room," she whispered.

So, so unbelievable. She wanted to go to his room. She wanted *him*.

She was running *to* him for once, not away.

"Are you sure?" he asked intently.

His heart nearly banged out of his chest for the few seconds it took her to answer.

"Yes." Then she was crying.

"Stop crying," he whispered thickly. God, was *he* going to cry again?

"I can't. I just can't believe—" She squeezed her

eyes shut then and would have turned away if he hadn't stopped her, held her.

"Believe what?"

She lifted her thick, damp lashes. Her gaze seared him right to his marrow.

"I can't believe you forgive me," Willa whispered. "I can't believe you…believe me. It's not just the past. There's the will, Otto, the house, everything. Yesterday, you thought I might be trying to con your grandfather, or something."

"I don't believe that anymore."

"I know." Her voice shook. "I've never had anyone who would just believe me."

Her gratitude left him staggered and humbled. And he wished he could take back the way he'd treated her when he first arrived. She wasn't crazy. She wasn't a thief or a liar.

Whatever had happened to create two wills, along with everything else that had happened that was so strange, it wasn't Willa's doing.

He realized in that instant how very alone she had to feel, and he didn't want her to feel that way now. He wanted to make sure of it.

"Don't worry about the will now," he urged her.

He kissed her gently, holding her. Needing her to believe *him*.

"I am so scared," she breathed against his lips.

"I'm scared, too. Does that help?"

He kissed her again, tasting the salt of her tears.

"Maybe," she said thickly. "Yes."

"We'll get through it together," he promised. He stood, swept her up into his arms, and carried her up those dark stairs to the light they could make together. Inside his room, he set her down and they stood there for a moment, neither of them speaking. It was surreal, that this was happening this way, in the middle of this nightmare.

It had been so long, and yet it seemed like no time had passed at all since the last time she'd been in his arms.

She belonged in his arms.

"What are you thinking?" she whispered, and she sounded scared again.

He told her the truth. "I was thinking that this would be the first time I've made love to you on a bed."

And she was silent, as if he'd taken her by surprise. He didn't always say the right thing, but he realized he had then. She was eager and shy at once, and the reminder that this wouldn't be the first time they'd made love helped set her at ease.

He went to her, placed his hand gently behind her head, and lowered his mouth to hers. She met him, her lips inviting, searching, willing.

He'd never wanted any woman the way he wanted Willa, and in a scorching burst of awareness, he knew one night would not be enough. Just the same as their time together in the past had not been enough.

There was no *enough* for him, with Willa.

Releasing her mouth, he traced a path with his lips down her chin, her neck, following the delicate line of her throat. She was wearing too many clothes, the heavy sweatshirt with a T-shirt under it, and jeans below that, but no way was he ripping them off in any haste.

This had to be slow, easy—gentle. And Willa had to know she could stop it at any time.

And he had to just pray she wouldn't.

She drew back, reached for his hand, pulled it up over her heart. He could feel her breast beneath the layers of clothing, feel she wore no bra, feel the hard, needy poke of her nipple.

Then she wriggled both arms between them and pulled the sweatshirt and T-shirt over her head, dropping them on the floor.

Her eyes shone at him, sexily shy, in the flicker of the candle. She was so lovely, his mind reeled. She looked like magic, a dream.

It was permission enough.

He scooped her up in his arms and took her to his bed where he laid her down gently, propped on his elbow beside her, and there was no sound but their breathing, the beating of their two hearts. He put his hand on the soft bloom of her sweet breasts and kissed her eyelids, her temples, her mouth again. He felt her need, her hunger, as he filled his hands with her, stroking, teasing those eager nipples as she pressed one then the other into his hand, then his mouth, moaning at the attention he gave.

"Willa…"

"What?" Her voice was a raspy plea.

"I need you."

She gave a half sob, reached for his shirt, tearing it over his head so that he had no choice but to pull back and help her remove it. She was already half sitting, unzipping her jeans, pushing them down her legs. He stood, helped her first with her own, then his.

Then, with one quick flick, she pulled away the little panties and she was nude.

Breathtakingly, stunningly, so trustingly nude.

He went back to her, and thinking became difficult, as did the gentle slowness with which he intended to make love to her. He lay beside her and her nipples waited for him, tight and greedy to his touch. He teased her breasts again, kissed her deeply, slid his hand down—down, to barely cover the soft center of her sexuality. She reached for him, tormenting him with the warm, firm feel of her fingers stroking him, rocking him with anticipation. He wanted to be inside her, but he also wanted to wait, even as need for her burned up every cell in his body.

Sliding in one finger, two, he probed her sweet, moist heat. She cried out his name and begged, and she nearly came undone right there. Her nails scraped his hair, his shoulders, his back, and then she did fall apart, so openly, so vulnerably, it blew his mind. And she shivered as if she were cold, when he knew it was the complete opposite.

She grabbed his face suddenly, her hands shaking, and kissed him hard, deep, longingly.

"Please," she whispered roughly against his mouth. "Please."

She reached between them, and he could have died right then. Her gaze, fierce and dazed at once, slashed into his.

His pulse hammered, and he ached with need. She wrapped her legs around him, reached again for the hard shaft proclaiming his hunger, and guided him home to her.

For a long beat in the shadowed, candle-lit room, he held her eyes, then he thrust all the way inside. She welcomed his hot possession, arching upward, and there was no reality left but the one in that bed with her. The whole world revolved around their two bodies joined together.

And he had just enough focus left in his brain to realize that he was irrevocably changed.

Everything he'd been pursuing meant nothing without a woman's love, and not just any woman's— Willa's. And even as it rocked him that he'd just thought of Willa in terms of love, he was sucked back in by the raw energy of her passion.

Her response was impossibly arousing, taunting, consuming. She alternately tore at the sheets and held on to him as if for dear life. She sobbed as she came again, and he had no choice but to go with her into that fire.

When he collapsed beside her and she reached, trembling for him, he held her tightly, their legs damply tangled, and he slept as he hadn't slept in fourteen years.

He had Willa again. At least for a night.

Penn woke to dead quiet. No wind, no rain. Just peace and a soothing sense of the world being right for the first time ever.

Then he remembered Marcus and all the sense of peace he felt disappeared. He opened his eyes, turned his head. Willa was already gone from the bed.

She was running scared this morning, he had no doubt. She'd taken a huge step last night, telling him the truth. He was haunted by that knowledge and all its implications.

He wanted her to have Limberlost; he knew that without any qualms. That meant he had nothing to start a business with, but he was not going to fight Willa for this farm. She and Birdie belonged here, and he—

Where did *he* belong? He'd thought he belonged in New York City. He could go back, find a new job. But that life he'd had didn't appeal anymore. He'd always wanted his own business. He'd quit Brown and Sons for that reason, thinking now was finally the time.

Maybe he'd been wrong about what time it was. He was free. He could do anything he wanted to do.

And right now he wanted to stay in Haven. Maybe

that was the time he hadn't even known had arrived. Life had come full circle, back to Haven, back to Willa.

Maybe they'd both been waiting for each other without even knowing it. Maybe this really could be their second chance.

If Marcus wasn't dead already, he'd gladly kill him with his own hands for what he'd done to Willa, and the ferocity of his need to protect her was almost mind-blowing.

If Marcus had indeed been here, hiding out, waiting for the moment he would choose to strike, maybe there was a vehicle, a working vehicle, around here somewhere. Maybe the water would go down enough today to get out of here in it. There was an old oil track that went up the other side of the hill to that pump house. Marcus could have left a vehicle there.

Why had Marcus waited? Why hadn't he killed Penn at the creek yesterday, if he'd had the chance?

Things didn't add up.

"The house wants everyone to stay right here," Birdie had claimed.

He didn't have the least bit of tolerance for the idea of any supernatural activity, but it was unbelievable how he could not get off this farm. And Marcus certainly hadn't had any control over the weather or his bad brakes....

And what had Marcus wanted, anyway? Willa had never told anyone the truth. If Marcus was worried that she would, surely he would have contacted

Willa, threatened her, a long time ago; but Willa said she hadn't seen Marcus in years.

If anything, as crazy as Marcus had sounded last night, he sounded guilty, too. *"You want me to pay?"* he'd shouted.

"Everybody's gonna die," he'd said, too.

He'd been trying to break down the door to get in. But he'd given up and shot himself.

A cold chill swept Penn. He sat up sharply, got off the bed and reached for his clothes. Last night everything had happened so quickly, too quickly, and the heartbreaking truth Willa had told him afterward had wiped everything else from his mind.

What if Marcus hadn't given up? What if he hadn't been here to hurt Willa but to save her? Because he felt guilty.

What if Marcus hadn't shot himself?

There was one way to find out, and he damned himself for not thinking of it last night.

Chapter 15

Willa splashed cold water on her face at her bathroom sink, then rubbed her cheeks red with a towel. She'd taken a shower. She had fresh clothes on. She had to be up and ready for Birdie. She had to be careful that Birdie didn't go outside or even open the front door. She had to hope and pray that they could get help today.

She could still smell Penn Ramsey all over her, feel his hands. See his gaze, so hot and hungry.

Somewhere in the middle of the night, she'd crept—run—from his bed. Thank God he was a sound sleeper. Fear throbbed in her stomach.

She hadn't expected it to be so good.

Not that she'd expected sex with Penn to be bad. But that good? She'd been sure her memories of their teenage lovemaking had to have been exaggerated in her mind. Nobody had sex that powerful, except in books. That was made-up stuff. And since sex had pretty much sucked for her otherwise...

She was sure the only reason it had been so good in her memory had to be some kind of filmy, sweet fantasy thing.

But, oh wow, it was not a fantasy, it had been very real. Very powerful.

Way past good.

What was also real was that sex was dangerous. People used sex to control others. Her stepfather. Marcus. Even Jared, to some extent. He'd saved her, so she *owed* him, and that included sex.

With Penn, sex was about desire, passion, aching hunger. She knew it had to have been good, in fact great, for him, too.

But there hadn't been any promises exchanged, and he had a life in the city, while she had a life in Haven. He'd said they'd get through whatever came of the will together, but she didn't really know what that meant.

He was just a ship passing back through her life, and he'd be gone again. What had happened between them last night was real enough, that was true, but anything beyond it was pure fantasy material. Even if he were to want something more, she wasn't ready. Trust wasn't something she handed out freely, not any more, not if she was going to be as smart as she told herself she was these days.

And she needed to get that straight in her head and deal with the situation accordingly, because that was where the danger lay with Penn—if she took this too seriously, or if she believed in this too much.

Or was she just running, again, the way she always ran? She hadn't given him a chance before, had she? Really given him a chance, with the truth and with her faith.

Was she doing the same thing now? Or just being smart?

He'd asked her for faith last night.

She met her own gaze in the mirror over the bathroom sink. Her skin was pale. There were tiny lines just starting to etch themselves around her eyes, her mouth, across her forehead. Her hair was still wet from her shower. She could see herself fourteen years ago, too. Wet and scared. There was always that scared look in those eyes she faced in the mirror.

God, she was tired of being scared, of hiding from everyone and, most of all, herself.

"Mommy?"

Birdie's little voice was followed by the doorknob turning. She hadn't locked the door. Birdie poked her sweet little face around the door.

"Can we have omplets for breakfast?" she asked.

No matter how many times she told Birdie it was "omelets," she always pronounced it "omplets."

"Okay, sweetie, sure." She rumpled Birdie's hair. Her little girl eyes always looked so huge when she wasn't wearing her glasses.

She went downstairs with Birdie, the little girl still in her Pooh Bear jammies and no glasses. She had to keep Birdie far, far away from the front door.

They all needed to get far, far away from Limberlost today, somehow. They needed help.

And here she was, fixing *omplets,* as if the world around her had not gone stark-raving mad.

But that was what she had to do, for Birdie's sake: act as if everything was normal.

Birdie clambered up on the stool while Willa pulled eggs and milk and cheese out of the fridge. Thank God the generator power was still going. She couldn't afford to lose anything, especially not food.

She hated to turn on lights, not wanting to stress the power supply, but the morning remained pale outside. At least it wasn't raining.

"Mama?"

"Yes?"

"I think Mr. Penn would be a good daddy, and it would be okay with me if you married him."

Willa turned around from the cabinet where she'd been about to pick out a mixing bowl.

"What?"

"I think you should marry Mr. Penn. He would be a good daddy for me. I like him."

Willa didn't know whether to laugh or cry. Birdie asked about Jared sometimes, but never had she mentioned wanting a new daddy. And this was not a good time to start.

"I'm not going to marry Mr. Penn," she said.

"I think the house wants you to," Birdie said.

"Birdie—"

"You love him, don't you?"

"Birdie!"

"The house wants you to!"

"The house doesn't want anything! You have to stop this, Birdie."

"But the house—"

"Right now, Birdie!"

Birdie bit her lip. Her eyes were so huge in her little face, and so serious.

Willa blinked back the emotion stinging at her eyes. She would have actually liked right then to think this was about children being more susceptible to supernatural activity. That would be better than the hurt of knowing it was about Birdie's need for a daddy.

She'd attached herself instantaneously to Penn, that was clear. He'd paid her a little attention and Birdie had soaked it right up.

Well, hadn't she done the same thing?

But she was a grown woman and she knew better

than Birdie. There was too much water under the bridge for her and Penn. Too much that was painful and could never be completely forgotten.

The house *shook*—and bowls clattered in the cabinet as she reached in. Willa's gaze swerved to the window over the sink.

It was dead still outside. No wind.

"Mama?"

She looked back at Birdie.

"The house is gonna get mad."

A chill crept up Willa's spine.

"Stop it, Birdie."

The house shook again.

"Mama—"

Birdie sounded scared now.

Willa looked outside again. Dread clogged her throat. Were they having another earthquake? There had been little tremors before the last one, too.

Just like this. Earthquakes were rare in West Virginia, and nobody in Haven had been prepared.

She didn't want to scare Birdie, though the little girl was scared already. She needed to find Penn.

"We have to get out of the house, Birdie. We don't have time for omplets."

"The house wants you to stay here! You and Mr. Penn! You have to do what the house wants!"

There was no talking sense to Birdie. "Stay here for a minute, baby."

She whirled, ran to the hall, and barreled straight into Penn.

"I need to talk to you," Penn said without preamble.

"We don't have time." Had he not felt the house shake?

"It's important."

There was a grim coldness to his features. She suddenly knew this was not about last night, not about them.

And he was holding Otto's shotgun.

"I think we're having another earthquake!" she cried. "Didn't you feel the house shake? We have to get out of here!"

His grim gaze didn't waver. "You can't go outside."

Her pulse kicked up another, more strident, notch. "Why?"

"That gun I took off Marcus is fully loaded."

"It can't be fully loaded. He shot him—" Her breath caught sharply in her throat. "You think Marcus didn't kill himself?"

"I *know* he didn't shoot himself. I should have checked last night."

She could see the self-blame in his hard expression. A lot had gone down between them last night. They'd both been in shock. She wanted to tell him not to blame himself, but she had a feeling it would do no good.

Mostly, she was scared.

"What does this mean?" She had to hear him say

it. Her head was reeling and she needed him to make sense of this for her.

"Someone shot him."

"Then someone else is on Limberlost! But…" She was still confused. "If someone is here, someone who wants to harm us, then why haven't they done it already?"

"The storm? Last night, it started hailing when I went outside to cover Marcus and get the gun. If someone was out there, they had to take cover."

The house shook again.

"There! Did you feel that?" She grabbed Penn's arm. "We can't just stay here, waiting. The house could fall down on top of us!"

"Mama?"

Birdie's voice came, plaintive and high, from the kitchen.

Willa turned around and hurried back to the kitchen. Birdie had jumped off the stool and stood in the middle of the room, backing up to the kitchen table, staring straight ahead.

"Mama," she whispered this time.

Then the house shook again, but it was not the whole house, just the kitchen, she realized.

And as she stood stock-still, something horrible clawing up her throat, she watched the kitchen drawer that had been stuck for so long shake right out of its hole and bang onto the floor.

She felt Penn behind her, his arms reaching around her.

"It's another earthquake," she breathed harshly. She looked back at Penn, horror in her shining eyes.

Nothing moved. No sound, in or outside the house.

The only thing that had shaken loose was that drawer.

"It's not an earthquake, Mama!" Birdie cried. "It's the house!"

The house wants us here.

Nobody moved for a stunned beat.

Then Willa knelt, reached for what sat in the drawer.

Penn came to look over her shoulder as she stood.

"It's an oil lease." Willa turned her shocked gaze up to him, then back to the papers. "Otto signed an oil lease on Limberlost."

Penn took the papers. "Short term. For exploration."

It looked like the oil company had only gotten a one-year lease out of him. Despite his age, Otto had still been too sharp to sign one for a longer term, until he saw the results of the exploration.

He peeled away the first page, looked at the second. It was another lease.

And the figures at the bottom blew his mind.

"They found more oil," Willa whispered. "Oh, my God. They're set to start drilling next month. Otto signed for it. He never said anything."

They both looked back at the papers, still stunned

by the figures. It had been a century since the gas and oil boom in these parts. The big companies had moved on, leaving their rusted wells and pump houses littered in overgrown backwoods to drill elsewhere, where it was cheaper and they didn't have to go as deep.

Now they were back. Recent exploration had been in the news, but Penn never thought it could be happening at Limberlost.

Otto had never said a word.

At least not to him and Willa.

Who had shot Marcus? Who was *left?* But he knew. Dammit, he knew. And it was unbelievable. *Marcus was her brother.*

"Jess," he said.

Willa whirled to face him. "What?"

"The only two people who benefit directly from this farm if you and I are gone would be Jess and Marcus. And with Marcus gone—"

"Jess? That would mean she had to k—"

She stopped. She didn't want to say it in front of Birdie.

He looked past her and his pulse fired.

"Where's Birdie?"

There was a scratching at the back door then the sound of a latch opening. Willa's heart hammered wildly and dread backed up in her throat.

She'd been distracted for a just a minute, but a minute was all it took.

"Birdie!" Willa ran.

Willa nearly tripped over the dog trying to get to the door.

But it was too late, she knew it was too late even before she reached it.

Birdie screamed.

Chapter 16

Blood roared in Willa's ears as she reached the back porch. Outside, beyond the covered porch, Jess clutched Birdie against her chest, a pistol pointed straight into the little girl's temple. Willa's head went light.

It was true. Jess had to have killed Marcus. She wanted the farm.

"Let Birdie go!" she cried. "You can't hurt her."

Birdie's terrified eyes shot right through her. She was sobbing now, and Jess shook her.

"Shut up!" Jess yelled at her.

"Let her go, Jess." Penn came up behind Willa. He had Otto's shotgun.

But he couldn't shoot Jess and risk Birdie.

"You can have the farm, Jess. We don't want it."

"I can't have it unless you're out of the way," Jess snapped back at him. "I told you not to come. You should have listened! Stayed in New York, just put it up for sale. Then I could have just bought it out from under you."

She knew about the oil. She had to know. But she also thought the farm had been willed to *him*. Guilt slashed him. She wouldn't be here, threatening Willa's and Birdie's lives, but for the fact that he was here. Otherwise, she would have just waited for them to move out after he'd sold the farm.

He had to keep her talking, that's all he could do for now.

"You can still have it. I don't want it."

Jess laughed harshly. "Right. And we'll just forget about this little incident."

"You mean the murder of your brother?"

"He was an idiot. He wanted to save her sweet little life." Jess jerked her head toward Willa. "He thought he owed it to her. Like Otto thought he owed her this farm."

She knew. Jess knew Otto had left her this farm. She knew about the two wills.

Then his brain stumbled back to what else she'd said.

"Why would Otto owe Willa anything?"

Willa's searing gaze wheeled to his. "I didn't want to tell you that," she whispered.

"He knew about that little slut and Marcus," Jess said. "Look how she finagled her way into the house with that old lie."

"Just let Birdie go," Willa begged.

He wanted to wring Jess's neck right there for saying the words he knew went straight to Willa's worst feelings about herself, but all that mattered now was that gun at Birdie's head.

"Why'd you wait so long, Jess? You've been hiding out here for days, haven't you? At the old pump house?"

"Stupid storm," Jess said. "I almost got you when I burned the barn down. Marcus showed up. Idiot drove as far as he could, then walked up. He knew about the oil. Poor fool, he was always looking for a buck he didn't have to earn. He started calling around, pretending to be Otto, until he found the company that made the deal on Limberlost. He thought the two of us could go in on it together, after we bought the farm. He had a conscience every once in a while, though. More the pity for him."

So she'd killed him. She was that cold.

There was nothing to keep her from shooting them all and being done with it.

And he was running out of ways to keep her talking.

"You can't get away with it," he tried. His fingers itched to raise the shotgun in his hand. But he was afraid if he so much as moved it an inch, she'd shoot Birdie immediately. "How are you going to explain all these dead bodies on the farm?"

"I'm not planning on making any explanations," Jess spat. "I'll head on out of here. I can get out the back way, out the oil road. I'll be terribly brave when the police call to let me know about the slaughter at Limberlost."

She clamped her hand over Birdie's mouth when the little girl started to scream again.

"I love you, sweetie," Willa cried. "It'll be okay."

She was lying. She knew it wasn't going to be okay.

The ground beneath their feet shook. Then Penn realized it wasn't the ground itself. It was the house behind them that had shaken the ground. *What the hell was going on?* Jess nearly lost her balance and he almost had the chance.

"You feel that, Jess?" he said. "There's another earthquake coming."

Willa's gaze wheeled back to Penn, shining.

"It's not an earthquake," she breathed. "It's the house. The house wants…"

Her gaze held his, trying to tell him something. He felt some strange buzz in the air suddenly. The ground shook again.

"The house wants us here," Willa whispered. "The house made us stay here. The house is protecting us. I believe it now."

"The house can't protect us," he said harshly. He

didn't take his eyes off Jess. She was grappling with Birdie and he knew, just knew, any minute she was going to be done and they were going to be dead.

"The house wants..." Willa blinked. "I love you," she said suddenly.

His heart boomed. *Now? Why did she have to tell him now?* When it was too late.

The house shook behind them again, and the ground trembled all around them. Thunder boomed, rocking his ears. Air swirled hard, and he felt his body ripped backward. He struck the wall with shocking impact, just as he saw something dark fly overhead, and all he knew was Willa's scream.

Willa hit the ground, blown backward by what force, she didn't know. She crawled to her feet, reddish fog blinding her for an awful beat. She stood there, stunned.

"Mama!"

She ran to Birdie's voice. The fog licked around her, then sharply swept back and away.

Birdie flung herself into her arms, sobbing, and Willa fell backward from the force of the little girl's clinging arms, her legs climbing around her mother. She held on and cried as Birdie buried her face in her shoulder.

Her mind reeled between joy and horror.

She pushed up, taking Birdie with her, looked over Birdie's head, dizzy and stunned.

Jess lay on the ground, a huge piece of metal roof

from the top of the farmhouse near her. Blood poured out from her head. She wasn't moving.

Cradling Birdie, keeping her from looking at Jess, Willa struggled to her feet. Penn! Where was Penn?

He lay slumped against the back of the house. New horror raced into her throat. Around them, the air was completely still. Bright light burst over them. It took her a confusing second to realize it was sun.

The sun was out.

Holding Birdie, she ran to Penn, dropped down to her knees, setting Birdie on the ground beside her, and reached for his face.

"Penn! Please, Penn!"

He didn't move. He didn't open his eyes.

"Penn!" She shook his shoulders.

Emotion tore through her when his eyes opened, then and he stared straight up at her.

"Thank God," she breathed roughly. "Thank God. I was so scared. Are you okay?" she half-sobbed.

She was crying and she didn't care. Nothing mattered, just Birdie and Penn, the two people she loved the most in the world. Alive. And the sun was out. Jess was gone, dead, as was Marcus.

It was what the house wanted.

The knowledge slid through her mind and she was too distraught to be scared of it. The house wanted them here. The house had protected them. Sometimes they hadn't done what the house wanted and the house had gotten angry, Birdie had said.

But the house had saved them—after she'd confessed the truth of her heart, when she'd stopped being scared.

There was no storm overhead. No earthquake.

Just the house....

Like Birdie had said all along.

"I'm okay," Penn said. He sat up, and she helped him, worried desperately. He was pale, but she couldn't see any injuries. No blood.

He was alive.

"Jess is dead," she whispered.

He stared across to where his cousin lay, to the huge piece of metal roof near her body.

"I know," he said. His intense gaze took hold of hers. "But we're alive."

She nodded, choking up again.

"The house is happy now," Birdie said. "See the sun, Mama?"

Penn's gaze didn't waver. "You said you love me," he said.

Willa swallowed thickly. "The house wanted me to say that," she said.

Her heart popped at the look in his eyes.

"I love you, Willa. And I don't care what the house thinks about it."

He wouldn't let go of her gaze.

She couldn't speak over the lump in her throat.

"Tell me you love me now, Willa," he said softly.

"What about New York?" she said, her voice thick.

"What about it?"

"You're going back to New York."

He shrugged. "Maybe I'll stay here."

"Why?" She didn't want him to stay here for her. She didn't want him to give up his dreams. "You always wanted to get out of Haven."

He shook his head. "I always wanted *you*, Willa." He looked up now, at that bright sky overhead then back to her. "I think the house wants me to stay here."

She saw the tease in his eyes now, but beneath it was something serious. He might or might not believe something supernatural happened here. But he believed in her.

"Mama," Birdie whispered, clutching at her arm suddenly. "Look, it's Black Beauty! She's back!"

And she was. There was her horse, munching grass at the edge of the woods as if nothing had ever happened.

She looked back at Penn and took a giant leap of faith, the one she knew he'd been waiting for. And after everything that had happened, it didn't scare her at all.

"I want you to stay here, too," she whispered, and she kissed him.

Epilogue

Three months later

The storm hadn't been anywhere near what they'd experienced at Limberlost for the rest of the Haven area. There'd been a few days of mild rain. No roads had been washed out—except for the road to Limberlost.

No power or telephone outages were reported, except theirs. It was as if the storm had been centered right over Limberlost, centered right over this house.

In fact, they almost could have believed they imagined the whole thing, except for the two dead bodies.

The police had found plenty of evidence at the

pump house to show Jess had been hiding out there, and the forensic fire team had uncovered proof that she'd torched the barn. Phone and oil company records tracked both Jess's and Marcus's impersonation of Otto and snooping into his financial dealings.

There had been plenty of questions about what had happened those two days at Limberlost, but Penn and Willa knew they'd never have all the answers.

The question of the will had been resolved when they sat down in the executor's office and he produced the will that was eventually probated. The will that was dated after both versions of Otto's will that Penn and Willa had had.

Otto had left Limberlost to them both, along with a letter asking them to forgive him for the past, and to forgive each other.

That final will was dated the day of the Haven earthquake. That night as that quake shook the ground and red lights burst over the farm, maybe, just maybe, something magical had been set in motion by Otto's wish.

Or not.

The town still whispered about that earthquake, about the perfect storm of atmospheric pressures that released positive ions that could trigger paranormal activity. There was a time when Willa had thought that was just so much hooey, but she wasn't sure now.

She might believe just about anything now, and even as Penn teased her about it, she knew he believed it, too.

They could have gone anywhere, either of them, with the money set to pour in from the oil company.

They resolved to stay at Limberlost. Penn would manage the farm and she'd have time, finally, to devote herself to her crafting business. With Penn's marketing skills, she'd start an online shop. It was good, all good.

Especially the part where they were all together at Limberlost.

"I don't think I can leave," he said. "The house wants me right here."

She wanted him there, too.

Sometimes, in the passing months, he told her the house wanted her to get a babysitter and go to the city for dinner and dancing. Other times, he told her the house wanted them to go swimming in the river, all of them.

Birdie liked to tell him the house wanted him to play Candyland ten times a day, and Willa told Birdie the house wanted her to clean her room.

Now, three months after that frightening morning when the sun had broken back over Limberlost, Penn told Willa, "I think the house wants us to get married."

His eyes on hers were bold, sweet and so true. Her heart filled her chest.

"Don't you think that's a cop-out?" she said. "What about you? What do *you* want?"

"I want to be with you forever, Willa," he growled, sliding his fingers into her hair, pulling her face up to his. "I want to marry you, Willa."

He put his lips on hers, soft, coaxing, and kissed her gently, tenderly. She felt that delicious, hazy heat she always knew with Penn.

"Well," she whispered when she pulled back to look into his hot, sweet gaze again. "I guess if it would make the house happy…"

"Is that a yes?"

She smiled hugely, and loved watching him smile back. Every day, the past seemed farther and farther away, and the future that much closer. But it was the present that mattered the most, and finally she'd learned to live in it, without self-recriminations, without the haunting memories, without the pain.

"Oh yes," she whispered. "It's a definite yes." Because she knew without a doubt that anything could happen in Haven.

Even a second chance at love.

* * * * *

*In honor of our 60th anniversary,
Harlequin® American Romance®
is celebrating by featuring an all-American male
each month, all year long with*
MEN MADE IN AMERICA!
*This June, we'll be featuring American men
living in the West.*

Here's a sneak preview of
THE CHIEF RANGER
by Rebecca Winters.

*Chief Ranger Vance Rossiter has to confront the
sister of a man who died while under Vance's
watch...and also confront his attraction to her.*

"Chief Ranger Rossiter?" The sight of the woman who'd stepped inside Vance's office brought him to his feet. "I'm Rachel Darrow. Your secretary said I should come right in."

"Please," he said, walking around his desk to shake her hand. At a glance he estimated she was in her midtwenties. Her feminine curves did wonders for the pale blue T-shirt and jeans she was wearing. "Ranger Jarvis informed me there's a young boy with you."

The unfriendly expression in her beautiful green eyes caught him off guard. "Yes," was her clipped reply. "When we arrived in Yosemite the ranger told me I couldn't go anywhere in the park until I talked to you first."

"That's right."

"Knowing you wanted this meeting to be private, he offered to show my nephew around Headquarters."

So this woman was the victim's sister.... "What's his name?"

"Nicky."

The boy who haunted Vance's dreams now had a name. "How old is he?"

"He turned six three weeks ago. Were you the man in charge when my brother and sister-in-law were killed?"

"Yes. To tell you I'm sorry for what happened couldn't begin to convey my feelings."

The woman's gaze didn't flicker. "I won't even try to describe mine. Just tell me one thing. Was their accident preventable?"

"Yes," he answered without hesitation.

"In other words, the people working under you fell asleep on your watch and two lives were snuffed out as a result."

Hearing it put like that, he had to set the record straight. "My staff had nothing to do with it. I, myself, could have prevented the loss of life."

Ms. Darrow's expression hardened. "So you admit culpability."

"Yes. I take full blame."

A look of pain crossed over her features. "You can

just stand there and admit it?" Her cry echoed that of his own tortured soul.

"Yes." He sucked in his breath.

"I work for a cruise line. Aboard ship, it's the captain's responsibility to maintain rigid safety regulations. If a disaster like that had happened while he was in charge he would have been relieved of his command and never given another ship again."

Rachel Darrow couldn't know she was preaching to the converted. "If you've come to the park with the intention of bringing a lawsuit against me for negligence, maybe you should." It would only be what he deserved.

"Maybe I will."

In the next instant, she wheeled around and hurried out of his office. Vance could have gone after her, but it would cause a scene, something he was loath to do for a variety of reasons. In the first place, he needed to cool down before he approached her again.

The discovery of the Darrows' frozen bodies had affected every ranger in the park. A little boy had been orphaned—a boy whose aunt was all he had left.

* * * * *

Will Rachel allow Vance to explain—
and will she let him into her heart?
Find out in
THE CHIEF RANGER
Available June 2009 from
Harlequin® American Romance®.

We'll be spotlighting a different series every month
throughout 2009 to celebrate our 60th anniversary.

Look for Harlequin®
American Romance® in June!

Join us for a year-long celebration of the rugged
American male! From cops to cowboys—
Men Made in America has the hero
you've been dreaming about!

Look for

The Chief Ranger

by Rebecca Winters, on sale in June!

---

www.eHarlequin.com   HARBPA09

Silhouette Desire

MAN of the MONTH

USA TODAY bestselling author

ANN MAJOR

THE BRIDE HUNTER

Former marine turned P.I. Connor Storm
is hired to find the long-lost Golden Spurs
heiress, Rebecca Collins, aka Anna Barton.
Once Connor finds her, desire takes over and
he marries her within two weeks! On their
wedding night he reveals he knows her true
identity and she flees. When he finds her
again, can he convince her that the love they
share is worth fighting for?

**Available June
wherever books are sold.**

REQUEST YOUR FREE BOOKS!

2 FREE NOVELS PLUS 2 FREE GIFTS!

Silhouette® Romantic

SUSPENSE

Sparked by Danger, Fueled by Passion!

Do you crave dark and sensual paranormal tales?

Get your fix with Silhouette Nocturne!

Silhouette®
Romantic
SUSPENSE

COMING NEXT MONTH

Available May 26, 2009

#1563 KINCAID'S DANGEROUS GAME—Kathleen Creighton
The Taken

Any time things get too difficult, Brenna Fallon runs away. So when private investigator Holt Kincaid shows up, wanting to bring her to her family, she buys time by asking him to find the daughter she once gave up. But when the child is kidnapped, Brenna must enter the highest stakes game of poker she's ever played as Holt searches for the girl, and both soon realize they're gambling with their hearts.

#1564 THE 9-MONTH BODYGUARD—Cindy Dees
Love in 60 Seconds

Tasked with protecting Silver Rothchild as she revives her singing career, Austin Dearing must also guard the baby she's secretly carrying. As attacks on Silver become more intense, she's driven into his arms, and their attraction is undeniable. But can Austin protect Silver enough to keep their romance from crashing to an end?

#1565 KNIGHT IN BLUE JEANS—Evelyn Vaughn
The Blade Keepers

Once he'd been her Prince Charming. But when Smith Donnell took a stand against his powerful secret heritage, he had to give up everything— including beautiful heiress Arden Leigh. When his past came back to threaten Arden, Smith had to emerge from the shadows and win back her trust—and heart—to save them both.

#1566 TALL DARK DEFENDER—Beth Cornelison

Caught in the crossfire of an illegal gambling ring, Annie Compton appreciates the watchful eye of former cop Jonah Devereaux, but she insists on learning to protect herself. As their attraction grows, they dig deeper into the case, danger surrounding them. They'll need to trust each other if they want to defeat these criminals.

SRSCNMBPA0509